I, Coriander

SALLY GARDNER

Orion
Children's Books

First published in Great Britain in 2005
by Orion Children's Books
First published in paperback in 2006
by Orion Children's Books
a division of the Orion Publishing Group Ltd
Orion House
5 Upper St Martin's Lane
London WC2H 9EA

5 7 9 10 8 6 4

ISBN-13 978 1 84255 664 1

Printed in Great Britain by Clays Ltd, St Ives plc

www.orionbooks.co.uk

In loving memory of an irreplaceable friend

Maria Björnson

*   *   *   *

The world we live in is nothing more than a mirror that reflects another world below its silvery surface, a land where time is but a small and unimportant thing, stripped of all its power.

I hope to find you there.   S.G.

Acknowledgments

I would like to thank from the bottom of my heart Jane Fior, for all her support, wisdom and brilliant ability to keep me on the right path and help me back after I had gone up several blind alleys; my agent Rosemary Sandberg for her encouragement over the years; my publisher Fiona Kennedy for her zest and loyalty; Lauri Hornik at Dial Books for her enthusiasm and commitment; and Judith Elliott, whose skill as an editor is quite incredible and who has picked up, spotted and shaken words and sentences that haven't been up to muster, always believing that I could go further than even I thought possible. Without her and Jane this book would have been pale by comparison.

Contents

PART THREE

PART FOUR

PART FIVE

PART SIX

PART SEVEN

Sweet Thames, run softly

till I end my song ...

Edmund Spenser *Prothalamion*

PART ONE

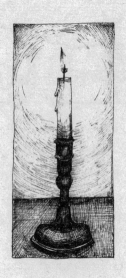

1

A Tale to Tell

*I*t is night, and our old house by the river is finally quiet. The baby has stopped its crying and been soothed back to sleep. Only the gentle lapping of the Thames can be heard outside my window. London is wrapped in a deep sleep, waiting for the watchman to call in the new day.

I have lit the first of seven candles to write my story by. On the table next to me is the silk purse that holds my mother's pearls and beside it is the ebony casket whose treasure I am only now beginning to understand. Next to that, shining nearly as bright as the moon, stands a pair of silver shoes.

I have a great many things to tell, of how I came by the silver shoes and more. And this being my story and a fairy tale besides, I will start once upon a time . . .

*M*y name is Coriander Hobie. I am the only child of Thomas and Eleanor Hobie, being born in this house in the year of Our Lord 1643. It is just a stone's throw from London Bridge, with the river running past the windows

3

at the back. To the front is my mother's once beautiful walled garden that leads through a wooden door out on to the bustling city street. The garden is all overgrown now; it has been neglected for too long. Once it was full of flowers and herbs of all description whose perfume could make even the Thames smell sweet, but now rosemary and nettles, briar roses and brambles have reclaimed it as their own.

It was this garden, the like of which no neighbours had ever seen, that first set tongues wagging. My father had planted it for my mother, and built her a pretty stillroom that backed on to the wall of the counting house. My mother in her quiet way knew more about herbs and their powers than anyone else, and together with her waiting woman Mary Danes she would spend hours in the stillroom, making all sorts of potions which were distilled and stored in tiny bottles. When I was small I used to hide under my mother's petticoats and listen to friends and neighbours as they brought their ailments to her like posies of sorrows, to be made better by one of her remedies. Later on, when I was too big to hide, they came to ask her other things, for by this time her reputation as a cunning woman with magical powers had spread as thistledown does, blown on the hot winds of gossip.

My first memories are of the garden and of this, my old bedchamber, whose walls my mother painted with fairy places and imaginary beasts. She wrote under each one in her fair script, and for every picture she had a story, as bright in the telling as the colours in which they were painted. When I was small I used to trace the letters with my finger, to feel how the spidery

4

writing was raised above the wood panelling, and I would say the names to myself like a magic charm to keep harm at bay. All the pictures, like the garden's blooms, are gone now, washed and scrubbed away. Only the faintest trace of the gold letters remains. They still shine through, like the memories.

I used to believe that my mother's life had started with me and that before I made my entrance into this world there was nothing. Nothing, that is, until the midsummer's day when my father, Thomas Hobie, first saw my mother standing under an oak tree in a country lane.

This is the story he told me, and the story I loved the best. When he was a young merchant with a head full of dreams, he put his hard-earned savings, together with what money his father had left him, into a ship bound for Constantinople, banking on her returning with a cargo of silk. Alas, news reached him that she had been lost in a great storm at sea, so that now he owned nothing but the clothes on his back.

In despair, my father walked out of the city and some ten miles into the country, on the chance of being able to borrow money from a distant cousin, a Master Stoop. When he arrived he found that Master Stoop had given up the never-ending struggle to live and had joined the ranks of the dead, leaving a wife and several small Stoops to be looked after.

My father had not the heart to ask for anything. Having paid his last respects, he set out mournfully on the road to London, resigned to his fate.

It was getting late when he met a strange-looking man with

a long beard tied in a knot, holding a lantern as round as the moon. The stranger told him he had been robbed by a high-wayman who had taken all he had owned, leaving him just the lantern. My father felt sorry to hear of this misfortune and offered him his cloak to keep the chill off. The stranger accepted it with thanks.

'Young man, to travel with an open and loving heart is worth more than all the gold coins in a treasure chest,' he said. 'Tomorrow your kindness will be rewarded.'

My father wished the fellow well and hoped that nothing more would befall him. Then he set off again, with only the light of the moon to show him the way. As he walked, a wave of tiredness came over him and he lay down to sleep.

Next morning he had not gone far when he thought he might be lost, for in the dawn light everything looked different.

At this point I, having heard the story so many times that I could repeat it to myself word for word, would interrupt and say, 'But you were on the right road.' He would laugh and reply, 'It was the road that would lead me to your mother, so how could it be wrong?'

To my childish way of thinking, it seemed that he met and married my mother in the space of one day. They arrived back in the city after the wedding to be greeted with the astonishing news that his ship had returned safe and sound with a cargo of fine silk.

From that day forward my father's life had been charmed with love and good fortune. No other merchant's ships fared as well. Untouched by pirates, wars or tempests, they sailed unmolested in calm seas, bringing back bounty fit for a king. Before long, my father was wealthy enough to be able to build this house for us by the river, where we lived in great luxury, having a cook and servants to look after us as well as Sam, my father's faithful apprentice.

It was no surprise to me that all this should happen so fast. It never entered my head to ask what my mother's family thought of their daughter marrying a young man who was penniless, or even if she had any family to mind. All these questions and many more besides only occurred to me much, much later when there was no one left to ask.

My father had two miniature paintings done of them both shortly after their wedding. My mother's portrait shows her wearing a cream gown beautifully embroidered and oversewn with tiny glimmering pearls. I imagine that this is how she looked when my father first saw her that midsummer's day under the oak tree. Wild flowers are woven into her hair and in her hand she is holding an oak leaf.

The background of this tiny painting always fascinated me. It is as if you are a bird looking down from a great height, seeing the land mapped out below. There, in a forest of oak trees, is a clearing in which there is a grand house with formal gardens. In the distance a tower stands tall over the trees, and I could just make out a figure at the top of the tower watching over the landscape, searching for something or someone. On the edge of the forest is a hunting party with dogs. Compared to the house and the tower, they look oddly large. A hawk sits on the outstretched arm of one of the riders. Another rider is standing up in his saddle blowing a horn. I looked at this painting many times before I spotted the white horse and the fox hidden in a thicket. For some reason that I cannot explain, their discovery worried me greatly. It gave me an uneasy feeling, as if somehow nothing was safe.

My father's portrait shows him looking young and hand-some. He is clean-shaven, wearing breeches and a linen shirt embroidered in the same pattern as my mother's dress. The scene behind him could not be more different. It is a view of a city with the river running through it like an opal green ribbon. You could be forgiven for thinking it a picture of London, except that the houses are brightly painted and mermaids and sea monsters can be seen in the water in amongst a fleet of tall ships with full-blown golden sails.

Even then, these two miniatures looked to me strangely out of time, as if they had been painted long, long ago in another world entirely. I know now what they mean. I know why my mother kept silent and why, at my darkest moment, her past claimed me, leading me back to something that could no longer be denied.

2
The Stuffed Alligator

I remember nothing of the trial of King Charles I. I
had no knowledge of what was meant by civil war. Such
great affairs in the tides of history passed me by. What I recall
is feeling safe and loved, the smell of my mother's perfume,
staying up late with my parents while they had their
dinner, going to sleep in my mother's arms. Of her kisses
I could tell you much. Of what my mother and father talked
about I could tell you little, except that it made them
sad.

In truth, I did not understand what momentous events were
unfolding or how they were to touch upon our lives. My world
revolved round smaller things. A stuffed alligator, a drowned
barber, a pair of silver shoes seemed to me just as strange as a
king losing his head.

That January day it was snowing, and the river had begun
to freeze over. I went running in great excitement to tell Danes
and found her weeping. This in itself was unusual, for Danes
was not given to tears.

It was nothing short of murder, she said, wiping the tears from her eyes.

'Who has been murdered?' I asked with interest.

'It is the King,' she replied. 'It is a wicked thing they have done, and no good will come of it.'

'Who has done what?'

'Oliver Cromwell and his axe man,' said Danes. 'Terrible! Who would think we would live to see our very own King have his head chopped off?'

'Did you see it?' I asked.

'No, no, but Master Thankless the tailor was there. He told me it was the saddest sight he had ever had the misfortune to witness. They held the poor King's head up high for all to see, and there was a groan from the crowd, the like of which London has never heard before. We live in dark days, my little sparrow.'

It being winter, I thought she must be right.

Danes blew her nose. 'The King is dead,' she said mournfully. 'Long live the King.'

'How can he be dead and alive at the same time?' I asked. It sounded a very hard thing to do.

'Because,' said Danes, 'his son Prince Charles is alive and well and he will, with God's grace, be the next King.'

It was a bitterly cold winter and snow had covered London in a thick white blanket, so that an eerie hush had descended over the city. The mighty water wheels at each end of the bridge had stopped their thunderous churning and huge icicles hung from them as the river slowly began freezing over. Old Father Thames looked as if he was growing a long white beard.

A Frost Fair was soon set up on the frozen river, with tented stalls selling all manner of wonderful things: gloves, hats, lace, pots, pans, needles, marbles, poppet dolls, spinning tops, spiced gingerbread, roasted chestnuts. The taverns did a roaring trade with food and ale, and late into the night I could hear singing and shouting outside my window, and smell hot pies tempting passers-by on to the ice.

Master Mullins the barber, who lived near us in Cheapside, was amongst the first to venture out on to the ice. He set up his small red-and-white-striped tent for business and called to his customers, promising them the closest shave in London. People watched the barber from the safety of the riverbank with awe, wondering if the frozen surface was to be trusted.

'Come!' shouted Master Mullins. 'It is as solid as a rock and could take the weight of the Devil himself.'

To prove his point he jumped up and down on the glassy surface.

'Master Mullins is a nincompoop,' said my mother as the Thames began to crack, and we watched all the other stall-holders take to the shore. Master Mullins refused to leave. When no customers would venture on to the ice to join him, he shouted to them from his tent, 'What are you waiting for? I have the best ointments in the whole city for thinning hair.'

Master Mullins became the talk of our street, not because of his ointments for thinning hair but for the way he plummeted through the ice, taking all his basins and razors with him.

I asked Danes what would become of him.

'The meddling old fool,' she said. 'He has most probably set up his tent at the bottom of the river and is already open for business and the spreading of gossip.'

After that I took to imagining Master Mullins cutting mermen's hair and trimming the whiskers of sea monsters. With that thought firmly in my head I worried no more about the barber, and my only regret was that he had not taken the stuffed alligator with him.

The alligator had been given to my father by a Captain Bailey, who had brought it back from China. He stood menacingly on top of the ebony cabinet in the study, the key kept safe in creamy white jaws with needle-sharp teeth.

I had always been fascinated by the treasures the cabinet held, shells in which you could hear the sea, a tiny turtle shell, butterflies with wings of brilliant blue. But the moment I saw the alligator I burst into tears, believing it to be real. It looked very angry and not at all pleased to be stuffed.

'It is only a baby alligator,' said my father, holding it for me to see. 'It will not bite.'

I would not go near it. I knew it was secretly waiting until we had left the room and then it would come alive.

This thought terrified me so much and gave me such nightmares that Danes would light all the candles to make sure that the alligator would not come in. She never said I was being a ninny, not once, and secretly I felt she was as scared of that alligator as I.

Winter finally departed and spring arrived, catching everyone by surprise. Windows were thrown wide open and carpets were taken outside and beaten, as if our house were a great blanket being shaken free of its fleas. Everything was washed and polished until the house smelt of lavender and beeswax, with bunches of fresh flowers filling the rooms. All our clothes were aired, our linens were cleaned and Master Thankless the tailor was sent for. New gowns were ordered and old gowns altered.

In amongst all this excitement a very strange thing happened. A parcel was left outside our garden gate. No name was written on it and there was no indication of where it was from. The mysterious package was brought inside and left on the hall table to be claimed. Every time I saw it sitting there I would feel a tingle of excitement.

Finally my mother opened it, carefully looking for any clues as to who might have sent it. Inside was the most beautiful pair of child-size silver shoes. They had tiny silver stitches on them and the letter C embroidered on their soles. I knew they were meant for me.

'Can I put them on?' I said, jumping up and down with joy.

My mother said nothing, but took the silver shoes over to the window to examine them. They shimmered and glimmered as if they were made out of glass. They whispered to me, 'Slip us on your dainty feet.'

'Please,' I said, pulling at my mother's skirts, 'let me.'

'I think not,' said my mother quietly. She took them back to the table and much to my surprise wrapped them up again.

Seeing them disappear like that was almost too much to bear. I felt my heart would surely break if they could not be mine.

'They are meant for me,' I said desperately. 'They have the letter C sewn on their soles. C is for Coriander.'

'I said no,' said my mother. Her voice had a sharpness to it that I had never heard before. It alarmed me, for I could not understand why such a wonderful present should make her so out of humour.

'I am sorry, Coriander,' she said, softening, 'but these shoes are not for you. Let that be an end to it.'

An end it was not. It was the beginning.

I felt the loss of the shoes like a hunger that would not go away. I knew they were still in the house. I was sure I could sometimes hear them calling me, and when I followed the sound it always led me to the door of my father's study.

As it turned out, it was not the alligator that I should have been scared of, but the silver shoes. They came from a land no ship can sail to, a place that is not marked on any map of the world. Only those who belong there can ever find it.

3

The Silver Shoes

Something changed in my mother after the silver shoes arrived. She seemed worried and would not let me out of her sight. Then another strange thing happened. I was playing in the garden. The Roundheads were trying to catch me so I had hidden out of sight under the garden bench: I had to, because I was a royal prince disguised as a girl. It was a good place to hide. No one knew I was there, not even the Round-heads, and this way I got to listen to all sorts of grown-up conversations, my mother having many friends and visitors who came to ask her for advice and remedies.

Honestly, I had no idea that the heart could cause such trouble and strife. It could be broken and still mend. It could be wounded and still heal. It could be given away and still returned, lost and still found. It could do all that and still you lived, though according to some, only just.

Mistress Patience Tofton was one of the visitors. I had not been listening that much until I heard the name Robert Bed-well. Then my ears pricked up, because I often played with his sons. They lived just down the river from us in Thames Street. He must, I supposed, have had a wife once and the boys a mother, but I had no memory of her.

Patience Tofton was all words and tears.

'He will be wanting a wife of letters,' she wept bitterly, 'a younger wife than me. I am too long a spinster.'

That was the silliest thing to say. Why, Master Bedwell was no spring chicken himself. He would be pleased to know that Patience Tofton, who was pretty, with fair hair and all her own teeth, should like him at all.

I peeped out from under the bench. My mother was talking to her kindly and softly, her words lost to me, and she kissed Patience on both cheeks.

'It will be all right, then?' asked Patience, getting up to leave.

I leapt out from my hiding place and said, 'Of course he will marry you! Do not take too long about it. Your two children are keen to be born.'

After I said it I thought perhaps I should not have. It took Patience Tofton by surprise, I can tell you. She went a greenish white, then fainted, falling like a bush that has been chopped down.

I went into the house, thinking it best to disappear until I heard the click of the garden gate. Then I looked out of my bedchamber window to see Master Bedwell helping Mistress Tofton home.

Later that day my mother came and sat on my bed.

'What made you say that to Patience?' she asked.

'I know not,' I said, for in truth I did not. 'I just know that she will marry Master Bedwell on Midsummer's Day and they will have a son and a daughter.'

'That is all?'

'Yes,' I said, giving it some thought. 'Well, that much I feel certain about.'

'Coriander,' said my mother, looking into my eyes, 'you are like me. But remember, you must keep your thoughts away from your tongue.'

'I will never say another word about any of the thoughts I have tumbling in my head,' I said apologetically.

'That would be a pity,' laughed my mother. 'Let us agree that you can tell them to me and your father and Danes, but no one else.'

'So can I have the silver shoes?'

'No, Coriander. Believe me, they are not the right shoes for you.' She sounded so sad. 'I had shoes like those once. I walked in them for seventeen years. I want you to have different shoes, shoes of your own choosing, not shoes that will take you where you should not be going.'

'But they are of my choosing,' I cried. 'I want them.'

'Oh Coriander, you are not old enough to understand,' said my mother. 'You must trust me. I know what is best for you.'

But what could be better than the silver shoes?

In our family much was made of the anniversary of my birth, and I was given presents to mark the day. This year my mother had arranged for us to take our barge upriver. I woke early on the day and lay in bed as the sunlight reflected watery shadows round my chamber, listening to the street criers as they made their way to the bridge. As soon as the watchman called the hour I ran down the corridor towards my mother and father's bedchamber. I felt like a top spinning with excitement.

'Today is my day! Wake up!' I cried. I pulled back the drapes on the huge oak four-poster bed and jumped into the middle of it.

'I know it,' laughed my father. 'And the street knows it too.' He leant down and brought out a box from under the bed.

I opened the box with trembling fingers. I was sure I knew what was in it. And there they were: plain, dead, heavy silver leather shoes. A sad imitation, a hopeless copy. Nothing like the silver shoes that had been left by the garden gate.

I felt tears welling up in my eyes and a lump in my throat.

'I am sorry, poppet,' said my father. 'You cannot have those shoes. We hoped you would be happy with these instead.'

I climbed out of bed, all the excitement of the day gone, fighting back tears of disappointment.

'Try them on,' said my mother.

I did. They hurt and pinched my toes. I turned to leave, feeling miserable.

'Coriander,' called my mother. I looked back into the bedchamber. The floor had become a sea and the bed a ship, seen from a great distance. I could hear their voices calling me from far away. It lasted a minute or less. Maybe I dreamt it. Maybe I did not. It was an image that came to haunt me, and I have often wondered what would have happened if I had done as I was told and left the silver shoes alone. Would everything then have been all right?

I made my way slowly and sadly back to my bedchamber, where Danes was waiting to dress me.

'Ah, what is the long face for, my little sparrow?' she said. 'Do you not like your new shoes?'

I said nothing.

'Oh well, you will not be wanting your present from me, then,' said Danes, taking out from her apron pocket a parcel tied up with silk ribbon. Inside was a sewing box in the shape of a frog, beautifully embroidered, with needles, a thimble and a tiny pair of scissors as well as a fabric book of all the different stitches. So thrilled was I that for a moment I forgot my grief over the shoes.

I was left alone with my little parcel while Danes went to attend to my mother. I could hear my father calling for hot water, and the silver shoes calling for me. For a moment I thought I must have imagined it, yet I could see where the call was coming from as if it were a wisp of smoke from my father's pipe. I got up and followed it down the stairs to the study.

'Coriander, Coriander, slip us on your dainty feet.
We are waiting, soft and silver, we will dance you down the
    street.'

I stood there listening, and finally I took my trembling courage in both hands and opened the door.

The study was dark. The alligator stood unmoving and all-seeing, king of the ebony cabinet, the key on its ribbon hanging out invitingly over his teeth.

I closed the door and stood with my back against it, my hand still on the handle, my heart beating like a drum. Quietness filled the room. There I stood. A decision had to be made. Did I have the courage to do this? I told myself that I did. I just wanted to see the shoes one more time, that was all.

I tried to move a chair over to the cabinet so that I could climb up and reach the key. The chair was far too heavy so I dragged it instead, as quietly as a chair can be dragged, then waited to make sure no one had heard me. I climbed up. Standing on tiptoe I was faced with the alligator. He looked more frightening close up, as if at any minute he would spring into action.

Did I really want to see the shoes that much? Oh yes, I did, and more. I half shut my eyes. Shaking with fear, I reached into the alligator's mouth and grabbed the key. If the alligator snapped his jaw shut I did not feel it, I did not see it.

I climbed down and opened the cabinet. Inside were many tiny drawers beautifully inlaid with cedarwood. I was not sure which one to choose.

I stood very still holding my breath and then I heard it again, this time no more than a whisper.

'Coriander, Coriander.'

I pulled open a drawer at the bottom and there they were, the most magical pair of shoes in the world. They were like glass. They were like diamonds. They were like stars.

Oh, I thought, what harm if I just tried them on?

The shoes fitted as if they were made for me. I stood marvelling at their beauty. How long I stood like that, I do not know. It must have been some time because to my alarm I heard my name being called, and not in a whisper.

'Coriander, Coriander! Where is the child?'

I quickly tried to take the shoes off, but they would not leave my feet. It was as if they were attached to me. In a panic of getting found out, I managed to close the drawer and put the key back into the alligator's mouth just before Danes opened the door.

'Coriander, what are you doing here, you ninny?' she said. 'We have been looking high and low for you. Come, the barge is about to leave.'

*T*he good thing about living by the river was that we had our very own water gate and mooring, so that there were proper steps down to our barge. Therefore there was no need to lift my skirt too high, and my shoes went unnoticed. I told myself that in the evening I would take them off and put them back, but just for today they would be mine.

We were rowed upriver past Whitehall, where the city gives way to open fields and pastures, the water losing its look of mercury and becoming clearer like the air. There in a meadow full of flowers our bargemen pulled the boat out of the river up on to the bank. Everyone then set to the task of making a day of doing nothing as comfortable as could be. Baskets of food were put under the trees, bottles of wine left to chill in the water and fishing lines set up for those in need of some sport.

While all this was going on I slipped away out of sight and sat down on a grassy bank, hoping that this time the shoes would come off. I pulled at them, and they slipped off with no trouble at all. I thought that I must have imagined they would not come off. I put them safely under some leaves where I knew no one would find them.

My mother too took off her shoes and stockings and, lifting her skirts, chased me round the meadow, her hair coming down, my cap flying off as we ran round and round until we fell in a heap of giggles. I made her daisy chains and found flowers for her hair. I paddled in the river, watched little fishes swim over my toes, was twirled like a windmill in my father's arms.

The day drifted past. It was time to retrieve my silver shoes. I was careful to keep my skirt well pulled down as we lay under the oak tree on an array of rugs and cushions like Roman emperors, eating our feast with dappled sunshine for our candles. My father had even arranged for three musicians to play sweet songs to us. In all this enjoyment I forgot what I had done until much later, when we were once more homeward bound.

The night rolled in over the river and stole the day away. The watermen lit lanterns on their boats so that the river twinkled and danced with lights. I was sleepy after such a wonderful day of fresh air and food.

My mother said suddenly and sharply, 'Coriander, where did you get those shoes?'

I was immediately wide awake and realised to my horror that my shoes were showing.

'I . . .' I stammered. I knew I was in trouble. 'I am sorry, but the other shoes pinched.'

'That was naughty,' said my mother, looking disappointed.

'You mean to say,' said my father, who had his arm round me, 'that you got up on a chair and put your hand in the alligator's mouth to get the key?'

I nodded.

'Well, well. I am impressed. Quite a brave thing to do for someone as scared of that alligator as you.'

My mother said nothing and looked away. I knew she was not pleased.

'Oh, Eleanor my love,' said my father, 'I know she should not have done it, but it is Coriander's day. Why not let her have the shoes and be done with it? I think she has earned them.'

'They are the best pair of shoes I have ever worn,' I said. I felt so excited that I hardly dared move in case he should change his mind.

My mother turned and stared at the shoes. 'They came off easily?' she asked me.

'Yes, they did,' I replied. I was not telling the truth.

'There. Perhaps we are just making too much of it,' said my father. 'What harm can come from a pair of shoes?'

My mother said, 'Plenty, and you know it, Thomas.'

4

Raven's Wings

I was still reeling from my triumph of having been given the silver shoes. My mother had said no more about them and I knew I had been forgiven. They were mine and that was all that mattered. I was determined to wear them the next day when I went with Danes on her usual errands.

'They will be ruined in all that mud and muck,' sighed Danes, tucking my hair into my cap and patting down my skirt. I was not going to say so, but I knew her to be right. My shoes were not suited to the rude streets of London.

'No, they will not. They are magic shoes,' I told her.

'Magic, are they?' said Danes, getting down the wicker basket from the shelf in the kitchen. We were going to take some potions to a cloth merchant's wife who lived in a house on the bridge and had had much trouble of late.

My mother came into the room with a bunch of herbs.

'You are not going in those shoes, my love, are you?' she asked.

'Yes,' I said stubbornly, 'I am.'

'They will be ruined.'

'They are never going to be ruined,' I assured her, 'because I put a magic charm on them this morning.'

'Do you not think,' said my mother, smiling and bending down, 'it would be better if you put a charm on them so that they always bring you safely home?'

We both looked at my shoes and studied them solemnly for a moment or two.

'Very pretty,' said my mother at last. 'I once –' she began, but then she stopped what she was saying and gave me a kiss. 'Off you go.'

It was, I remember, a pleasant spring morning with the promise of heat. The narrow street at the front of our house was full of people bustling and jostling, making their way towards the bridge. I held tightly to Danes's hand. Not being very tall, all I could see were skirts and legs coming towards me and pushing past me. Hawkers, apprentices and watermen were shouting. Then into the mix of noise and people came a gaggle of hissing geese. They sounded like a hundred fish-women arguing over the price of their wares. I pulled on Danes's apron and begged her to carry me. I found geese worrying.

'Oh, you are too big for this, Coriander,' she chided, lifting me up on to her hip so that I could see where we were going.

When I was carried I liked to stretch my arms up high to see if I had grown tall enough to touch the signs that hung down from each house and shop. They were all painted with different pictures so that you could see who lived where and who sold what. Our house sign was a painted mulberry tree. The signs were supposed to be hung high enough for a horse and rider to pass beneath. In our narrow street some signs were so low that I thought a rider might lose his hat, if not his head.

Finally we came to the bridge. 'You can walk from here, little sparrow,' said Danes, setting me down and straightening herself out.

This is the one and only bridge that goes over the River Thames. There is no other way to cross it unless you go by boat. It is the most splendid bridge. I loved and feared it in equal measure. I feared the pickled heads stuck on poles at Traitors' Gate like monstrous gargoyles staring down on the travellers, warning them what could befall such vagabonds and Royalists in this godly city. I loved the bustle of the shops, the street hawkers, the street criers, the overhanging gardens, the walkways. There was, so my father said, no bridge in the world to match it.

By the time we arrived the shops were all open. Coaches and carts rumbled along the main thoroughfare, scattering passers-by and chickens. The noise was deafening, with church bells ringing out, apprentices shouting, the water wheels churning. People were scurrying this way and that, not looking where they were going. Into this human soup came the beasts from the countryside on their way to the cattle market.

I was sure that if I were to let go of Danes's hand I would get lost, be swept away in the sea of people. Usually this thought made me cling to her like a limpet. Except today. Today was different. Today I was wearing my new silver shoes. In truth, in spite of my charm, I was more worried about my shoes getting dirty in the mire than of getting lost.

In front of us, an argument had broken out between a candle seller and a woman leaning out of the third storey of a nearby house. The street trader was very wet and smelling none too sweet, and he was accusing the woman of emptying a pisspot over him.

'Why did you do that?' he yelled. 'The river is just behind you. The bridge is a thoroughfare for decent God-fearing people, not the local midden.'

The woman shook her fist and banged her window to. I hoped no one else felt in the mood for emptying chamber pots, and tightened my grasp on Danes.

'Watch where you put your feet,' she said.

I looked down and saw that my shoes were shimmering like a heat haze on a hot day. I pulled my hand away from Danes to lift up my skirt so that I could have a better look.

'Danes,' I said. 'My shoes!'

There was no answer. An eerie mist had descended. Danes, like everyone else on the bridge, had disappeared. All was silent.

I felt so scared that I could not even cry out. I stood very still and closed my eyes tight shut, hoping that when I opened them everything would be as it was before. I waited, then dared myself to peep. The mist had lifted and I found myself standing quite alone outside a shop whose sign was a painted mirror. I thought that I should go in and ask for help. The strange thing was that I had this thought and found myself in the shop all in the same moment. It was gloomy and cool inside and it took a little while for my eyes to adjust to the darkness. When they did, I saw, to my horror, that standing on top of the counter was a large midnight black raven.

My instinct was to run out of the shop, but my shoes would not or could not move. The raven watched me, its pearl black eyes glittering in the darkness.

'Do not be frightened,' said the raven. 'She is waiting for you upstairs.'

I nearly jumped out of my skin. Uncertain what to do, I looked at the door I had come in by. The raven, as if reading my thoughts, flew up, blocking my exit. I could feel the power of its outstretched wings as a wave of feathery darkness swooped down towards me. My heart by now was fair fit to burst with fright. I ran for my life up the stairs, terrified lest he should follow me.

'Please let Danes be waiting for me,' I prayed. 'Please.'

I knew the moment that I entered the room that I was lost, unbearably lost, for there was no Danes, just an old woman sitting in a chair looking at herself in a gilded mirror. The room was panelled in wood; there was a fire in the grate but the flames were still, as if painted. The leaded window was partly open behind the old woman. Shining shards of light were thrown in different directions across the wall and floor, and I could just see the river outside. There too nothing moved: not the river, not the boats, not the people, not the seagulls suspended in the air. All was silent without wind or breath, as if time was being held back by an invisible hand.

All I could hear was my heart pounding.

'Come, my child,' said the old woman in a croaking voice. 'Do not be frightened. Let me take a good look at you.'

I wanted to run out of the room, but my shoes refused to move. The old woman was somehow much nearer than she had been a minute before. She had small eyes and a hooked nose and a mole on her chin. Her face was like a mask.

'Do you know me?' she asked. And for a moment the mask became transparent and another face of cruel beauty shone through. Which of these two faces frightened me more I could not say.

'No,' I said. I tried to back away from her, but still the shoes refused to move. It was then I noticed that somehow the raven had got into the room and was perching on the back of her chair.

'How old are you?' asked the old woman.

'Six summers,' I told her.

'So young, so young,' she whispered.

I stared down at my feet. The oddness of everything made me think of Danes, and tears began to roll down my face. The old woman seemed neither moved nor worried to see me so upset.

'The shoes suit you very well indeed,' said the old woman.

'I am glad you like them. You do like them?'

I said nothing. All the words I had in me seemed frozen to my tongue.

'Cronus,' said the old woman, 'do you think she likes the shoes?'

'Why, of course she does,' said the raven. 'She chose to take them.'

I was now sobbing so much that my chest was heaving and my shoulders shaking and I wondered if I would shudder apart. I felt hot and light-headed. Finally I found my voice and gasped through my tears, 'I want to go home, please. Now.'

The old woman smiled and held up the gilded mirror for me to see. The glass was made of liquid silver that whirled round and round. It was like looking into a deep, deep well: I could fall into it and be lost for ever. My head felt as if there was a thunderstorm crackling in it.

The old woman studied me closely. 'What do you see?'

'Nothing,' I said miserably. 'I want to go home.'

She put the mirror face down. 'Where is home?'

I told her.

'Your mother, how is she?'

All the time the old woman had been speaking I could hear my mother's sweet voice saying over and over again, 'Take off the shoes, take off the shoes.' I sat down on the floor and pulled at them with all my might.

It was as if I were lost in a forest and being hunted like a wild animal. The room began to spin and a high-pitched

sound flooded into my head. Then all was silver and all was
darkness.

'*A*re you all right?' said a voice somewhere near me. I
looked up to see the friendly face of Master Thankless
the tailor.

A crowd of people had gathered round us on the bridge.

'Lucky you saw her,' said a passer-by.

'Ain't she the cunning woman's child?' said another.

'I don't feel well,' I whispered.

'You don't look too bonny,' said Master Thankless. Gently
he lifted me up and carried me home. I wanted to tell him that
I had lost Danes, but my head was pounding and lights were
flickering before my eyes, and I was afraid that if I opened my
mouth I would be sick.

The last thing I remember him saying to me was 'Where are
your shoes?'

5

The Heat Within

I thought I saw the raven's outstretched wings beating at my windowpane, was sure that I heard his brutal cry in the night. I thought I saw the old woman watching me from a tower across the river. I know that I saw Death standing by my door holding his huge scythe, waiting for someone. Was it me?

How long the fever lasted I could not tell, for all things tumbled together, the dark and the light becoming one.

My mother was with me, that much I am sure of. So was Danes. She said over and over again, 'Do not fly away, my little sparrow.'

The heat outside. The heat in the room. The heat in my body. So much heat that it was hard to breathe. I was propped up in bed and given a bitter brew to drink, and my burning, itching skin was soothed with ointments. I was moved at some point to my mother and father's chamber and lay in their bed, the windows open in hope of a cooling breeze, but the air was slow and stagnant. I could hear the cries of the watermen, 'Westward ho, eastward ho,' the bells of St Magnus, St

George and St Saviour's ringing out, the screeching of seagulls. The shouts of the street sellers were the background noise to my fevered nightmares. The room would start to melt away and I was once more in a forest. I could hear the hunter's horn, I could see the shadows of the dogs as they came chasing after me, I could feel their hot breath on my neck. I would wake screaming, feeling my energy ebb away from me like the sluggish river tide.

It was at the darkest of moments, when my sight was so bad that I could hardly make out my mother's face, that I first saw the fairy. She twinkled and danced in the shafts of sunlight that struggled between the drapes at the window. I could not be sure if it was really a fairy or just the stuff of dreams. Yet every time I woke, there she was floating above me. She became my good luck charm. I felt that as long as she was there, I would be all right.

When I was better and the shutters were folded back and the drapes removed, I saw for the first time that what I had taken for a fairy was in truth a beautiful poppet doll that Danes had sewn for me while I lay there so ill. She was made out of cloth, with tiny stitched fingers and feet. She had red hair like good Queen Elizabeth and a ruff that looked like wings. I called her Beth and felt not the least bit disappointed that she was not real. I told no one but Beth about the raven and the old woman with the mirror. I thought no one else would believe me.

Master Thankless came to call, bringing me presents of ripe cherries and some pretty marbles. I was still too weak to stand, my legs being as thin as twigs, and during the day I lay on a bed in the garden, under the shade of the crabapple tree.

'How are you doing, little mistress?' Master Thankless asked cheerfully. 'You gave us a fright.'

'I am much better now,' I said, showing him Beth.

'Beautiful! Did you make her?'

'No,' I laughed. 'Mistress Danes did.'

'Well, mistress,' said Master Thankless, 'you could come and teach my apprentice a thing or two.'

Danes blushed. 'It is nothing.'

'We have a lot to thank you for, good sir,' said my mother.

'That's funny,' I giggled, 'a lot to thank Master Thankless for.'

'I have fun made of my name more times than I can say it,' said the tailor good-naturedly.

'Oh,' I said, 'I did not mean …'

'Of course not,' he said with a smile. 'Bless you, it is good to see you looking so much better.'

After a while, my mother excused herself, leaving Master Thankless with Danes to discuss the new clothes that needed ordering.

'I am glad to be making the little mistress another gown,' said the tailor, smiling at me. I went on playing with Beth while, thinking that I was not listening, he leant forward and whispered to Danes, 'Forgive me for asking, but I am baffled as to what really happened on the bridge.'

'So am I, Master Thankless,' said Danes. 'The bridge is a

dangerous place. Why, only last week twelve sheep ran wild and rushed into the river, taking the printer's apprentice with them.'

'Yes, yes,' said the tailor. 'But how did the little mistress get separated from you in the first place? And how did she lose her shoes? One moment I saw you both standing there outside the haberdasher's and the next she was gone. When I found her, the child looked as if she had seen a ghost. And the state of her! It seems impossible for it all to have happened so quickly.'

'I think, good sir, you make too much of it,' said Danes. 'To me she was lost for quite long enough.'

'Nay, mistress, that is the odd thing. It was not that long, I do assure you. My apprentice, Gabriel Appleby, witnessed it too and will say the same as I do,' said the tailor, quite distressed.

'Surely all that matters,' said Danes firmly, 'is that you found her, for which we are eternally grateful. The rest is of no importance.'

'Forgive me for saying it,' said Master Thankless, 'but there is a lot of talk, and not all of it favourable.'

'So I have heard,' said Danes. 'One would have thought that people had better ways to spend their time than in idle gossip.'

My keen ears heard every word that was said, and every word worried me greatly. I had long wanted to ask what had happened to the shoes and could not, because I felt that in some way I was to blame for what had befallen me: that if I had done as I was bidden, I would never have got lost, never have become ill, never have had the nightmares.

'Quite so,' said the tailor. He continued in almost a whisper, 'But they are saying it was –'

'Well, Master Thankless,' said Danes, 'it is for the Good Lord to know the answer.'

I was not sure if I had heard him right. It was only when Danes stood up quickly that I realised what he had said.

Danes sighed. 'We should be used to it by now. Nevertheless, it rubs me up the wrong way.'

The word that he had used was sorcery. I did not know what it meant, but as I repeated it to myself I had a feeling of foreboding.

*T*hat summer was the beginning of my love of words and stitches. My mother taught me my letters with great kindness and patience, under the crabapple tree.

There is an art to using a quill and it took me many sheets of paper and much spillage of ink before I could write my letters. I hated it when the pen splattered, which it often did, stubbornly ruining my hard work. Though when it went well, the words gathered on the paper like flowers in a meadow on a sunny day.

I got through so much ink in the learning that the inkseller took to knocking at least once a week on the garden door. He had a grey solemn face that looked as if it was chiselled out of stone; he was stooped down like the letter C, as if he were

Atlas carrying the weight of the world in his wooden barrel of ink. Maybe he did. I have learnt that there is great power in words, no matter how long or short they be.

'Is this for you then, young mistress?' asked the inkseller, as he carefully poured his ink through a funnel into a stone jar.

'Yes, of course,' I said with pride.

'Well, there's a thing going to waste, all that learning on a girl,' said the inkseller.

My father thought it was good that I was being taught to read and write, and said that I had a quick wit which would serve me well in life. He taught me the countries of the world on his globe, and showed me maps that had Neptune sitting on a rock looking out over his vast watery kingdom of mermaids and sea monsters.

My dear Danes could neither read nor write, and had no wish to learn. Instead she could sew with the fingertips of fairies, her stitches so small and delicate that her needle could embroider whole stories. I would sit for hours with her trying to do the same, but without much success.

When at last I was strong enough there were plans to send me out of London to Highgate with Danes, for the good country air. I was to stay with the sister of my father's long-dead cousin Master Stoop, who had married a rich man, a Master Gearing. In truth Beth and I were not looking forward to it. I had never been away from home and Highgate was quite a distance.

On the eve of my departure, Mistress Gearing turned up.

She was dressed as plainly as any woman I had seen and I wondered if she was very poor. My clothes and my mother's had embroidery and fine lace, but Mistress Gearing wore a simple black wool skirt and jacket with a starched white apron and a plain white collar. Her hair was pulled back and hidden under a cap with flaps hanging down that made her look like a startled rabbit. She held a huge nosegay of flowers in which she buried her face and stayed with her back against the garden gate, refusing all requests to come further in.

The whole thing seemed most vexing and I had determined by this time that I was not going to spend a month in the country with a badly dressed rabbit, no matter how good the air might be.

'Did you come by carriage?' enquired my mother.

'Nay,' replied Mistress Gearing, 'I walked with purpose and God for company and shall go home the same way, with the Lord's blessing.'

'I will not hear of it,' said my mother. 'You must be footsore. Why, you are most welcome to stay with us for tonight. My husband has already arranged a carriage to take Coriander and Danes to Highgate tomorrow.'

'Go on,' Danes whispered to me, 'go and greet her. She is probably shy and unused to the ways of the city.'

'No, no,' shouted the rabbit as I went up to her. 'No, keep your distance, I pray!'

'Mistress Gearing,' said my mother kindly, 'there has been some misunderstanding. I would not have dreamt of asking you to have Coriander if I thought she was still sick.'

'I have heard that the child had a deadly disease,' said Mistress Gearing, sniffing so hard at the nosegay that she was overcome with a fit of the sneezes.

Then she let the truth of it out, all her words tumbling and stumbling over one another.

'I wish I could say that she had been saved by the Lord's providence, but strange rumours have reached us about your household, and my good husband asked me to come to say that he believes it is fairy lore and sorcery that has healed the child. We are God-fearing people and want no part of the Devil's work.'

'Come, mistress, what is this?' said my mother.

Mistress Gearing put her hands up in front of her. My mother could contain herself no longer and burst out laughing as Mistress Gearing ran out of the garden gate and up the street.

My father did not think it funny.

'Thomas,' said my mother, 'she must be a very silly woman.'

'She did not want me because she thought I had been made better by the fairies,' I piped up.

'What nonsense,' said my mother.

My father's face was grave.

'It is no laughing matter, Eleanor my love.'

'Thomas, do not look so solemn. Do you not think the woman a fool?'

'I think you must be more careful, Eleanor. Please, for my sake and Coriander's.'

His voice made me feel uncomfortable.

'The old world has been washed away and a new order of fools is here. Have a care, my love. They bring with them an unforgiving Lord.'

6

The Pearl Necklace

I was nine summers old when my happy, carefree world was torn apart and turned upside down.

It happened one cold wintry morning in January. I had been sitting in my mother's bedchamber looking out of the window and up into the heavy sky. All it had to do was snow and then I would be able to go sledging with Edmund Bedwell. He was now twelve years old and his brother thirteen. Their father had married Mistress Patience some three years back and they had a new baby brother as round and plump as a sweet plum pudding. Now both the boys were studying at St Paul's School and I was most envious of them. I could read and write well, too, and had a hunger for knowledge.

Edmund told me grandly that learning Latin and Greek was too hard for the feeble mind of a girl.

'What about good Queen Elizabeth?' I said, putting my hands on my hips and trying to look very grown-up. 'She was taught all those subjects and more besides.'

'That is quite different,' said Edmund. 'She was a princess, not just an ordinary girl like you.'

'That matters not. It shows that girls can do as well as boys,' I said firmly.

'You will be a merchant's wife and have a large house to run,' said Edmund. 'Better to be taught housewifery. Then at least you will be useful to your husband, as Mistress Patience is to my father. Let the men worry about the Latin and Greek.'

Sometimes Edmund annoyed me much.

'Do you think,' I asked my mother, as I wrote my name on the frozen windowpane, 'that girls have feeble minds?'

'Did Edmund Bedwell tell you that?' she laughed.

I nodded.

'You have a very bright and lively mind, and long may it be so. Master Edmund Bedwell is a nincompoop. Now, tell me, my pretty, what necklace shall I wear today?'

'That is easy,' I said, 'the rose pink pearls.'

She smiled. 'A good choice.' She held them up to the light and looked at them. 'This was the first present your father ever gave me. Come, tie me a pretty bow.' She handed me the necklace.

'Why are the pearls cloudy when they are not on your neck and clear when they are?' I asked.

'The heat from my skin warms them up and they become clear,' said my mother, brushing back my hair from my face. 'You have, without doubt, the tightest show of red ringlets I have ever seen.'

'I wish I had hair like yours,' I said.

'Save your wishes. You are going to be a beauty one day, my sweet Coriander.'

Danes came clattering into the room with a tray of hot chocolate and a plate of sweetmeats.

'Forgive me,' said Danes, putting the jugs and china bowls out on the table, 'but Mistress Mullins is downstairs and wishes to speak to you on a personal matter and Mistress Potter is here again with her old problem. Lord, will that woman never be satisfied?'

'Now, now,' said my mother, smiling. 'Let us be kind. Tell them I shall not be long.'

I sat down and poured the chocolate for my mother and me. Danes took the tray and went away.

My mother shivered as she closed the door. 'It is cold in here. Is the window open?'

I got up and at that moment something dark and feathery flew hard against the glass, shattering it. My mother was still standing by the mirror. Suddenly she made a gasping sound, and I turned round to see her put a hand out to steady herself. What happened next was like a dream. The pearls round her neck broke free and poured down with a hard tip-tap like raindrops, bouncing up only to hit the wooden floorboards again. Then my mother's eyelids fluttered and closed as she began to sink, her skirts billowing beneath her like the sails of a ship. The pins that held her hair in place came loose as she went down. She landed with a deadening thud as her head hit the unforgiving floor, her arms stretched out, her hair a golden sea of waves. I tried to catch her, knocking the hot chocolate off the table, the china bowls breaking, spilling their dark creamy content so that it spread across the floor, bleeding into my mother's dress.

A cry, a terrible cry broke the silence. It seemed to be coming from me. I saw the door fly open and watched in horror as Danes and two servants did acrobatics in the air, tripping and tumbling over the pearls like high wire walkers, dancing for balance.

My father rushed into the room. He too slipped, then regained his footing, his face ashen white. He lifted my mother on to the bed and loosened her clothes. While I stood watching, the pearls rolled noisily across the floor under the furniture and out of sight. I knelt down and collected as many as I could. All I could think was that as long as they did not cloud over everything would be all right.

For four days my mother lay still and without words, veiled in a deep sleep. None of her own remedies made her any better. Finally, much against Danes's advice, my father sent for the doctor.

Doctor Turnbull had been skulking outside like a river rat, knowing that in the end my father would give in. I had never liked this man. He was dirty, with long greasy hair, and he smelt of sickness. He brought with him two skinny, sulky apprentices weighed down with jars of leeches and other instruments of torture. He tut-tutted at all the potions Danes was using and ordered that the room be heated to pull the fever out. Then he set his black leeches loose on my mother's fair skin to bleed her, and he would allow nothing to be given to her except what he prescribed.

Danes was banned from the room and Doctor Turnbull took delight in whispering to my father that she had made his patient worse.

My father, red-eyed and pale with worry, said nothing.

'Send him away, sir,' Danes pleaded. 'Please, for the love of Eleanor, send him away.'

'No, I cannot, not if there is the smallest chance she could be saved.'

'Please,' begged Danes.

It was not to be. The doctor stayed.

Mistress Patience came to sit with my mother, as did Master Bedwell. A steady stream of friends and neighbours came to pay their respects.

My mother got worse. She looked as pale as the sheets, and still the doctor insisted he could cure her. His last resort was to cut my mother's hair off and put two dead pigeons at her feet.

'What have you done, you buffoon?' my father cried in horror when he saw her.

'I had occasion,' said Doctor Turnbull, seeing my father's ferocious face, 'to bring down the fever of a lady by this very treatment.'

'You are a fool, and this,' said my father, pointing to the dead pigeons, 'is no better, sir, than witchcraft. Nay, worse, for it is done in the name of medicine.'

'I have never been so insulted in all my life,' said the doctor.

'More's the damn pity,' said my father, and he ordered the doctor and his apprentices out of the house.

However, as the doctor left, death came creeping in. The pigeons were removed and Danes made my mother as comfortable as she could. That night the room was lit with a single candle and at some time I must have been carried back to my own bed, for I was woken in the early hours of the morning by the roar of a wild animal. My heart leapt with fright and I could make no sense of where the noise was coming from, except that it seemed to be inside the house. I rushed out of bed and into my mother's bedchamber. My father was howling as if his soul was breaking. Danes gathered me up in her arms.

'Your mother is dead, my little sparrow,' she said.

And so the first part of my tale is told, and with it a candle goes out.

PART TWO

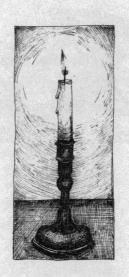

7

The Shadow

Six bells ring out to let the parish know that a woman has died, followed by a bell that tolls once for every year of her life. Thirty-three bells rang out for my mother.

My father ordered all the windows of our house to be opened so that her spirit could find its way home. A mournful wind came whistling in, wailing its woe into every room, blowing out all the candles and bringing with it drizzling fog that hung about the house long after the windows had been closed again.

Danes washed and perfumed my mother as lovingly as if she were in an enchanted sleep, dressing her in a plain white shift and covering her shorn head. She looked so still and beautiful, her skin as white as candle wax, her hands folded together holding a winter rose from her garden. Black crape was hung round the bed and at the windows. All the paintings and mirrors were turned to the wall. Mourning clothes and cloaks were ordered from Master Thankless and mourning rings were bought. She lay in the great oak bed for three days, my father at her side, weeping inconsolably and saying over and over that she must be left there, she was just sleeping, she still might wake.

It was as if my world had fallen down, as if the house had lost its walls. I woke up in the morning, I went to bed at night as if I were someone else, someone without thought or feeling.

On the day of the funeral my father was almost wild with grief. His apprentice Sam dressed him and helped him down to our barge as if he were an old man unsteady on his feet. No coffin had been ordered; my father would not hear of it. He wanted my mother's body to go back into the earth and replenish it. She would have wished it.

It was then that the whispers and rumours grew louder, for it was thought most shocking that my mother was not to be buried in a churchyard. This confirmed the neighbours' worst fears, that she had been a stranger, with airs and graces that did not belong in this world.

It was dusk by the time we set off, and stillness was over the water. The sky was a bluish black and flakes of snow were falling. No one accompanied us. No priest, no mourners, just me, my father and Danes, the four bargemen and two servants. My mother's body was placed on the barge wrapped in a white winding sheet. Silently we made our way upriver, the ripple of the water and the rhythm of the oars the only song that was sung. Past Whitehall, out of the city into the countryside, back to the meadows she had loved.

In the gloom it bore no resemblance to the place we had

visited so long ago. Here I had danced with my mother under a canopy of leaves, the grass full of wild flowers. And there, where she was to be buried, her grave a raw wound in the earth, was the spot where we had kept our food baskets cool from the midday sun.

We each held a torch, a light against the gathering darkness, the white of my mother's shroud the only thing that could be seen clearly.

'We are but shadows that have a short time dancing in the light,' said my father, tears running down his face. 'There never was one as lovely as thee. Go free, my love, and one day we may be together again. Amen.'

He threw a rose down into the grave.

'We live to die, we die to live eternally.'

As he said these words, I heard a loud cawing sound and looked up to see a raven perched high in the oak tree above us, its shape outlined dark against the night sky, its cry shattering the stillness like breaking glass. My father took hold of my hand and pulled me closer to him so that I was hidden by his mourning cloak.

By now it had started to snow heavily. Two gravediggers covered the grave until the earth lay flat and even. We stood there frozen with the cold. Only when the meadow had turned white and the grave was lost in the new snow did we make our way back to the barge. I shivered as I heard the raven's haunting cry bidding us farewell.

The barge made its way back downriver on the outgoing

tide. Black water. Black barge. My mother had taken with her all the colours of the rainbow.

*I*t was as if that day we buried not only my mother but a part of my father as well, for the man who now sat in his room refusing to eat looked nothing like the strong and powerful father I knew. His face was gaunt; he had cut off all his long hair so that it stuck out in tufts. He did not shave and seemed hardly aware of anyone's presence.

The house was now mine to roam. I could do what I liked, but all I wanted was for my mother to be there. Joan, the cook, having no food to prepare, sat in silence at the kitchen table. The servants were hardly to be seen. It was as if the whole house was cast under a spell. Danes seemed as bewildered by my mother's death as my father.

Two cold and dreadful months passed. The black crape was still draped in every room. The sheets on the great oak bed were still unchanged and every day my father placed another winter rose on her pillow. He would allow no one to touch her dresses or her jewels.

I was beginning to think that this melancholy state would go on for ever when one evening Master Bedwell came to see my father.

I had been sitting with him in the living chamber, both of us staring silently into the fire. I was telling myself a story about a princess and a dragon. My father, lost in his thoughts, was jolted back into the present by a servant announcing

Master Bedwell's arrival.

'I am not in,' said my father. 'I will see no one.'

'I need to talk to you,' said Master Bedwell, brushing the servant aside. 'This cannot go on.'

'There is nothing to say,' said my father, turning back to look into the fire.

'There is a great deal that must be said. I would like to talk to you in private,' said Master Bedwell.

I got up to leave, but my father took hold of my hand and sat me down beside him.

'Well?' he said.

'I have come on an important matter,' said Master Bedwell, looking at me uncertainly.

'You may speak freely,' said my father.

Master Bedwell started to walk back and forth in front of the fire and then addressed himself to the flames, where most of our thoughts seemed to be that evening.

'You have enemies and there is much talk.'

'There has always been talk,' said my father angrily. 'I know people say Eleanor was a cunning woman, even a sorceress. Men cling like drowning sailors to the hope of a life everlasting and a forgiving Lord. Then, if that fails to bring them comfort, there are always magicians, sorcerers, witches and fairies to blame for their misfortune. Blame everyone and everything but do not blame yourself. What fools are men!' My father's laugh was hollow.

'Cannot you see that we are living in dangerous times?' said

55

Master Bedwell, opening his arms wide. 'Gossip flies. All this could be taken away from you tomorrow and you would be left with nothing.'

'What more can anyone take from me?' said my father, his head bent down. 'Everywhere I go I carry my hell with me.'

'I know, and I am greatly sorry for it, but I am talking of worldly matters. A word in the wrong ear could be catastrophic for you. Oliver Cromwell is confiscating the wealth of those who supported the Royalist cause, and you have never made any bones about the fact that you think the King should never have been beheaded. And now there is this bad business at Worcester.'

I knew about Worcester from Danes. She had told me that Oliver Cromwell had defeated the newly crowned King of Scotland, Charles II, there. The King himself, with a price on his head, had escaped to France.

'What are you suggesting I should do?' said my father.

'Marry again. Marry a good Puritan woman.'

'What! Eleanor is barely cold in her grave,' said my father.

'Nobody can replace Eleanor. I know that. But you could find a woman with whom you could rub along and who with her piety would stifle gossip. It would allow you to keep your wealth and your home. I have connections in Bristol who could help you.'

'This is folly!' cried my father, getting up and striding over to the window. 'I am not a Puritan! I have no sympathy with their cause.' He pushed his hands angrily through his hair and turned to face Master Bedwell. 'Do you really believe that they would take this all away?' he asked.

'Without hesitation, my dear friend. You have heard what befell Master Needham. He has been made bankrupt. He too was a self-made man with no connections in Parliament, no relatives to help him, no link with the Puritans. We are in the midst of a terrible storm and I fear that it can only get worse,' said Master Bedwell. 'For pity's sake, think before you lose everything.'

That night I went to bed feeling uneasy. I woke to find that the window in my room had blown open and the rain was pouring in. I had to battle to close it and still the window rattled like a skeleton shaking its bones. Lightning flashed and I felt sure that I could see demons and alligators crawling across the walls. My heart pounded as I pulled the covers over my head. I wished my mother were there to make everything all right.

I could not get back to sleep, so I got out of bed and went on to the landing. Looking down, I could see my father's study door open and warm light shining into the cold, gloomy hall. Holding my breath, I tiptoed down the stairs, hoping with every creaking step that he would come and rescue me.

I stood by the study door and looked in. My father was sitting at his desk. In front of him was an ebony casket inlaid with tiny stars that glittered in the candlelight. I had never seen it before and was curious as to what it held. I went closer, expecting at any moment that my father would look up and ask what I was doing, but when he did raise his head, he seemed to look straight through me as if I was not there.

I stood beside him and looked in the casket. At the very bottom was something silver, as insubstantial as gossamer. Carefully I put my hand into the casket and touched it.

I nearly jumped out of my skin when my father said suddenly, 'I should have given it back to her.'

'What should you have given back to her?' I whispered. He still had a faraway look in his eyes.

'Her shadow. She gave it to me on our wedding night and told me to keep it safe. She said that if I ever returned it, she would have no choice but to leave and we would be parted for ever.'

I stood staring at the shadow as it shimmered restlessly at the bottom of the casket. A dull light shone from it. It awoke in me a distant memory of a mirror I had once seen.

'Now I do not know if I did the right thing,' continued my father. Then he cried out louder, 'Oh Lord, did I do the right thing?'

I asked as softly as I could, 'Father, was my mother a fairy?'

My father looked up and, as if seeing me for the first time, said, 'What are you doing here, Coriander?'

'I was woken by the wind and I was frightened,' I said.

He looked down at the casket and closed the lid quickly.

'How long have you been standing there?' he asked.

'Not long. Is that really a fairy shadow?'

'It is nothing. The casket is empty,' said my father curtly.

'But I saw . . .'

'Nothing,' interrupted my father. 'You saw nothing. You heard nothing.' Then he added softly, 'Nothing but a fairy tale.'

8

What Will Be

I wish I could unpick the stitches of time that have become all tangled and twisted together. If I could have done that, my mother would still be here and everything would be all right. But everything was not all right, and I wondered now if it ever would be again.

Some months after her death my father came back from Bristol saying that he had met a godly widow called Maud Leggs, and it was arranged that come next Wednesday they were to be wed.

I wanted to say 'Wait, please wait,' but the look on his face told me this would be unwise. Since the loss of my mother, my father had become a cloudy man, given to sudden changes of moods and temper: a ship on a rough sea, blown by invisible storms, his maps and stars lost for good. Danes called him a man under an evil spell.

The day of the wedding arrived. My father was as much out of sorts as the rainy weather, finding fault with the smallest details. His water was not hot enough, his shirt was itchy, his shoes were too tight, his servants were too slow, his coffee was too cold.

So it went on until finally Master and Mistress Bedwell came to accompany him to church. I would dearly have liked to go with them, but my father thought it unnecessary, as it was just to be a simple service. He refused to have anything made of the wedding, saying that it was unseemly to do so. This set tongues a-wagging, confirming that my father had something to hide. 'The sooner it is over the better,' he said to me as he left.

I stayed looking out of the window with Beth, my beloved doll, waiting for them all to return.

It was raining quite hard when the garden gate finally opened and my father came in with a large, shapeless lady who waddled like a goose, followed by a string bean of a girl who looked awkward and ill at ease. My father ushered them quickly into the house where the wedding party stood in the hall shaking the rain from their cloaks and hats. Servants rushed around busying themselves, taking away the wet outer garments and giving the party something to talk about as they were left standing there, like an ill-matched group of figures in a painting.

My stepmother was no beauty. She was round and squat with a face not unlike a potato that had been scrubbed. She had deep pockmarks and a thin scar of a mouth, two tiny beady eyes and a small upturned piggy nose given to sniffing and snorting. She smelt of sour milk. Her voice told me that she was not city bred.

'Ah,' said my father, relieved to have something to say. 'This is my daughter Coriander. Coriander, this is Mistress Maud Leggs and this is her daughter Hester.'

'Don't you mean Mistress Hobie, sir? I am your wife now,' said Maud, smiling at him and showing an odd assortment of black teeth.

My father looked taken aback at her words, as if a spell had been broken and the truth of what he had done had only now occurred to him.

My stepmother looked down at me and said, 'Coriander, that be a fancy name.'

'It is a name dear to my heart,' said my father. 'It was given to her by her mother.'

Maud scrunched up her nose disapprovingly, and sniffed. 'It is not a Christian name.'

My father, ignoring her, carried on. 'This is Mistress Mary Danes, who runs the house.'

I could see clearly by the way she looked at Danes that this did not please her one bit. There was an uncomfortable silence.

'Come,' said Master Bedwell, hastily taking Maud's arm, 'I am sure you are hungry. You have been on the road for a long time, I hear.'

'We came with God's blessing and His grace,' said Maud.

'Quite,' said Master Bedwell, leading her into the dining chamber.

Hester stayed in the hall.

'How old are you?' she said quietly.

'Nine summers. And you?' I asked.

'Twelve summers,' said Hester.

'Hester,' shouted her mother so loudly that it made us both jump.

'What have I done?' said my father when she had gone. He stood looking longingly up the stairs as if waiting for someone to appear.

'It will be all right,' I said, trying to move him towards the dining chamber and the guests.

Master Bedwell came out into the hall again. 'My dear neighbour, we are all waiting for you.'

'What on earth made you think she was a suitable wife for me?' said my father.

'She was introduced to me when I was last in Bristol, by a very fine lady who understood your situation,' said Master Bedwell, patting him on the back. 'She felt that Mistress Leggs would match your needs perfectly. You must give it a chance. It is the soul that matters, not the outward appearance. What did Oliver Cromwell say? Paint me, warts and all?'

'What care I what anyone said? I should never have done this,' said my father.

'Perhaps it is all for the best. At least Coriander will have someone to play with and it shows the woman is not barren. One day, you might have a son.'

'With her?' said my father.

'Come,' said Master Bedwell, taking my father firmly by the arm, 'let us join the others.'

*T*he wedding breakfast was eaten in silence, all small talk having long since run out. Maud looked round the room, which she pronounced not being to her liking. As for the pictures that hung on the walls, in her view it was better that walls had naught upon them than paintings that could lead to unseemly and ungodly thoughts.

'Well,' said Master Bedwell, who was doing his best to keep the company going, 'a new mistress, a new broom to sweep the house clean. I am sure there will be some changes. Why, when I married my dear Patience . . .'

'Too many mirrors,' interrupted Maud. 'The Good Lord never used a mirror.'

I wondered how she knew that, and I was about to ask when Patience, in hope of changing the conversation, said, 'Coriander is learning Latin and Greek.'

Maud looked affronted, as if a full chamber pot had been emptied at her feet.

'I am a plain woman and I speak my mind as God finds it. What use is there, I would like to know, in any girl reading?'

'Surely,' said Master Bedwell good-heartedly, 'it is a very —'

Maud interrupted him again. 'I can neither read nor write, nor would I allow any girl of mine to meddle with letters. I believe that women's minds are too feeble for such things, and words only confuse them the more. Nay, I will leave the reading of the Bible and such matters to the greater minds of men.'

My father was now drinking the wine as if it were water.

Maud squinted and looked at me. 'Reading and fancy

names do young girls no good, just give them ungodly ideas.'

After that there was nothing more to say.

We all waited to be released like parishioners at a Sunday service when the sermon has gone on for too long. At last Master Bedwell coughed, saying he was sorry to break up such a happy gathering, but Patience, being big with child, needed to rest. My father, by now a little unsteady on his feet, insisted on seeing them out, and pulled me with him.

'I should never have done this. I feel I have been duped,' he said to Master Bedwell when we were in the garden again.

'It will be all right,' said Master Bedwell reassuringly.

'We have nothing in common. What will we say to one another?' said my father, holding tight on to his arm.

'Give it a chance,' said Master Bedwell. 'It is for the best, my dear friend.'

My father watched Master and Mistress Bedwell as they got into their carriage and drove off. Slowly he closed the garden gate, and taking my hand he said, almost in a whisper, 'I am sorry,' and for a moment, just one moment, I saw my other father, the kind and gentle man who would whirl me in his arms like a windmill, who laughed and loved. A tear rolled down his face. He sniffed and wiped it away and we returned slowly hand in hand to the dining chamber to find Maud sitting with her daughter, her plate piled high.

'Furniture, my good husband,' she said, her mouth full of food, 'that be too pretty is without pure thought. Tables with turned and carved legs only encourage the Devil to dine.'

My father stared at her, bewildered.

'This house needs to be made ready for the second coming of the Lord Jesus Christ, for when he returns to our fair city and takes his rightful place as king, he'll be needing a good meal in a godly home. Do you not agree, husband?'

My father was speechless. Maud, in no way put off by his silence, said, 'He will be very hungry. It has been a long time since the Last Supper.'

My father made a choking noise and went to the table. He refilled his glass and swigged the wine back in one gulp.

'So,' said Maud, crossing her arms over her ample chest and shaking herself like a hen before it lays an egg, 'there will be changes in this house.'

At first I thought Maud quite silly, and that nobody apart from Hester could possibly be frightened of a woman who believed in such stupid things, like saying the Lord Jesus never laughed or that all girls had feeble minds, but I soon came to see that for all her nonsense, there was a dark side to this new stepmother of mine.

Over those first few weeks she busied herself like a fat ferret, snooping and sniffing around, looking into every corner with her beady eyes. My chamber she disapproved of the most, because it had pictures that did not feature Bible stories and had too much gold leaf and too many words.

'I think it be pretty,' Hester whispered to me.

Maud, whose ears missed not a sound, turned on her

daughter. 'Did the Good Lord ask you to speak?'

'No, Mother,' said Hester, cowering.

'Then hold your tongue,' said Maud, and she slapped Hester hard across the face. 'A thorn in my side, that's what you be.' She bustled off to examine a piece of silver on the sideboard.

'Are you all right?' I asked.

Hester nodded. 'I am always doing the wrong thing or saying the wrong thing or standing in the wrong place.'

Maud turned round again.

'Be silent,' she said, pulling Hester away from me, 'or I will with the Lord's blessing see fit to strike you again.'

*T*here were only two chambers that my new stepmother could not enter. One was my father's study, and this caused her much frustration. The other was the stillroom. Maud did not notice it until the weather improved and she was able to turn her attention to my mother's garden.

'All these fancy flowers that have no respect for the Lord will have to be dug up,' she said, waddling out one late spring morning. 'We will replace them with good Christian plants that have honest English names.'

'I think you should ask the master before you dig anything up,' said Danes.

Maud took no notice. She went over to the stillroom and stuck her face against the glass until her breath clouded up the windowpane.

'What have we here?'

'It was my late mistress's stillroom,' said Danes.

'It is just as I thought, a place for the Devil to make his potions and charms. Where is the key?'

'The key is with Master Hobie,' answered Danes.

'Do not fib to me,' said Maud. 'You have got that key.'

Danes repeated what she had said, whereupon Maud started to push and bump at the stillroom door with all her might.

'Shall I get the master?' asked Danes.

Maud stopped her banging, out of breath.

'There is no need to trouble my good husband. This is a matter we womenfolk can sort out.'

'I think you will find that the master may well have something to say about you breaking down the stillroom door,' said Danes calmly.

Maud was now as angry as a buzzing hornet. Hester backed away while Maud stamped her foot and banged her chubby fists once more upon the door. At last she gave up and dragged Hester back towards the house.

'Well, Hester, what do you think?' she yelled.

Hester stared down at the floor as if all the words had fallen out of her.

'The Good Lord give me strength, to be plagued with such a dim-witted child,' said Maud.

Hester, looking terrified, said nothing.

'Strange, do you not think it be strange,' said Maud, shaking her fist, 'strange that a wife be not allowed into her husband's study, strange that the stillroom be barred from her? I think it more than strange.'

Hester flinched.

'I tell you the Devil himself waits in that garden in the guise of a serpent,' Maud spat out.

'Do not say that, Mother, I beg of you,' said Hester, trembling with fear.

Maud let her go and turned round to face Danes. 'I say that there be witchcraft going on in this house,' she said with a sniff.

Hester made a whimpering noise.

I stood there amazed at all this talk. There was no serpent in our garden, only herbs and flowers that could help to make you well again.

'What are you staring at?' yelled Maud, turning to me.

'Nothing,' I said.

'Do you know where the key is?'

'No,' I said.

'Come here, you little . . .'

Danes stood in front of me, pulling herself up to her full height so that Maud could not get hold of me. 'Maybe you should rest, mistress. You are out of sorts. I will ask the master to call the doctor.'

My stepmother sat down heavily, her legs spread out, her body slumped like a huge roll of unwound fabric.

'I do not need your meddling,' she said. 'Get out, you witches both. I know what devilry you are up to now. Bringing on my toothache, that's what.'

We left the house before my stepmother had a chance to change her mind. We could still hear her infernal bawling from the street.

Danes walked with such purpose that I had to run to keep up with her. I hoped that perhaps we were going to see my father to tell him the truth about Maud, for I felt sure that if it had not been for Danes I too would be feeling the full force of her anger.

To my surprise Danes made her way to the tailor's shop on London Bridge.

When we arrived, Gabriel Appleby, Master Thankless's apprentice, was helping a lady with a large parcel into a sedan chair.

'What can I do for you, good mistress?' said Gabriel cheerfully.

'I need to speak to your master alone,' said Danes.

'Certainly,' said Gabriel, taking us through the shop and up the small wooden staircase that led to Master Thankless's living quarters.

'Mistress Danes, how good to see you,' said Master Thankless. Then, seeing the look on her face, he said, 'Mistress, are you all right? You look pale.'

'I must ask you a favour,' said Danes. 'You have been so good to us in the past and once more I have to lean on your good nature and ask for your help.'

Master Thankless sat us down and fetched some wine and sweetmeats.

'How can I be of service?'

'As you know, we now have a new mistress. Nothing is right with her. Now she claims to believe that the garden is the work of no lesser person than the Devil.'

'Surely not!' said Master Thankless.

'As for the stillroom, she says it is where charms and potions are made. She has already demanded the key and I believe that she will not hesitate to destroy all my mistress's potions once she gets inside, believing them to be the stuff of witchcraft.'

'Oddsfish, what is the world coming to!' said Master Thankless. 'I will gladly keep them for you, mistress. I have a good dry cellar to store them in. It would be terrible if those remedies were to be lost. Why, in the past I have often been cured by one of those tiny bottles, as have many of my friends and neighbours.'

'The new mistress is a Puritan with strong beliefs.' Danes moved her chair closer and whispered to the tailor, 'There is something not right in all this. A dark riddle that I do not understand.'

I got up and went to look out of the window down into the busy street below. That was when I first saw the crooked man. He was dressed all in black and was standing in the doorway of a shop across the street. His tall hat was tilted back and round green glasses hid his eyes, but I sensed that he was looking straight at me and I felt a shiver go down my spine. Danes says when that happens someone has walked over your grave.

'Tomorrow then,' said Master Thankless.

'Bless you,' said Danes, getting up to leave. 'Come, we must be getting home, my little sparrow.'

I looked down again.

The crooked man had vanished.

9

The Power of Bindweed

*M*y stepmother was like bindweed that grows where it is not wanted, slowly spreading its sticky tendrils over everything. She had been in our house for nine months and I had counted every moment, every hour, every day. Little by little she smothered all the joy out of my life, leaving only dullness and sore knees. For there was a lot of praying to be done, a lot of hard pews to sit on, a lot of sermons to be heard, and much thanking of the Good Lord. Thanking Him for my stepmother I found very hard to do, so I thanked Him for Danes instead.

The only room that still sang of days long gone was my bedchamber, with its painted walls shining with magic.

'What do the pictures speak of?' asked Hester one day when we were alone there.

'They are fairy stories that my mother used to tell me,' I said. 'Would you like to hear one?'

Hester nodded, so I told her the story of the princess who was locked up in a tower by a wicked witch, and rescued by a penniless tailor who tricked the witch into becoming so small that she could fit into a thimble. Hester laughed when she heard this.

When I had finished she asked nervously, 'Where is God?'

'He is not in these stories. These are fairy tales.'

Hester thought for a while. 'Do you think God minds fairy tales?'

'I do not know. Maybe not,' I said. 'Maybe, if your mother is right about Him. According to her, He seems to disapprove of much.'

Hester looked again at the pictures on the wall.

'I wish that were not so,' she said sadly.

Hester was used by her mother as a whipping post for all her ill humours. Maud kicked and beat her whenever the mood took her and, believe me, it took her often. Once or twice she tried to lash out at me, but Danes was having none of it.

When my father was around my stepmother was goodness itself, holding on to her Bible and asking my father if he would be so kind as to read it to her. The passages she liked the best all had to do with floods and plagues of locusts and rivers of blood. If there was a good killing then my stepmother looked happy, enjoying every minute of the misery God's people had to endure.

'This,' she said one day, clutching the Bible to her bosom, 'is the very history of England. It foretold our past and will foretell our future.'

I was not so sure, but knew better than to say so.

My father seemed to be wise in the ways of avoidance and would sit most evenings eating his dinner in silence, his head to one side as if listening to what my stepmother was saying. In truth, I think he was miles away, his mind drifting far out to sea.

It was only when she started to interfere with Danes that my father spoke up. 'Mistress, you will leave things alone. I like them as they are.'

My stepmother was much affronted. No doubt she thought she had married a man who had lost his tongue, one who would agree to anything. A silent man can seem many things until he opens his mouth.

'I was only putting things away, articles I knew Jesus would find unbecoming,' she said.

'For the time being,' said my father coldly, 'I would prefer it if the house was fit for me and mine. When Jesus comes, *if* he comes, then by all means let him take down the paintings and move the furniture.'

'All I do is for the comfort of your soul, good husband,' said my stepmother in a small hurt voice. 'I work night and day to make you a godly man and prepare your house for the Lord.'

My father sighed, then, taking up his pipe and his papers, retreated to his study.

My stepmother, much vexed, watched him go. 'I will be mistress of this house,' she muttered under her breath. 'And no witch's servant is going to stop me.' That is what she called Danes, for as far as my stepmother was concerned Danes was the root of all evil.

*M*atters came to a head one washday.

Twice a month, Danes took our laundry by barge across the Thames to the wash-house in Southwark. She would stay there for the best part of the day to make sure that it was all cleaned to her satisfaction. The linen would come back beautifully pressed and folded and smelling of lavender.

My stepmother decided that there was no need to send the laundry away so often and that it should be done at home. She stubbornly refused to take any advice from Danes, and so it was that on the wettest Monday of the month, when it had already rained for three days without stopping, the washing was begun. Since there was no place for it to dry, the soaking sheets were draped over banisters and suspended from beams. The house looked like a market stall covered in wet linen.

'Why does it not dry?' said my stepmother, stamping her stumpy feet on the ground while wet sheets dripped around her as if the rainclouds from outside had come indoors for warmth.

'Mistress,' said Danes politely, 'the custom is for the laundry to be taken away and returned clean and dry. It has never been done like this. The master would not like it.'

'How dare you tell me what the master would or would not like! I tell you it be a waste of good coinage when we have so many idle servants to hand,' shouted my stepmother.

Later that evening when my father came home he was not best pleased to see the wet sheets dripping down the stairs on to the floor below. He was in an even worse humour when he found that there was no supper to be had because Joan had been too busy boiling pans of water.

'What is the meaning of this?' he said. 'Have we sunk so low that we take in washing?'

'No, good husband,' said my stepmother. 'I thought not to waste your coin and to undertake the washing here in the house.'

'Mistress,' said my father, 'will you please heed the advice of Danes on the household management. She has run this house from the beginning. Surely you have enough to do without bothering yourself with laundry.'

'If I have offended you, my good husband, may the Lord smite me down,' said Maud, and much to my delight He did, with toothache. The pain was so bad that she stayed in her bedchamber.

'Is she going to die?' I asked hopefully.

'Nay, I doubt it,' said Danes.

After two days of moaning and groaning my stepmother demanded to see Doctor Turnbull. This time my father did not hesitate to call him. I was delighted to see the old river rat again and only hoped that he had brought his friend and helpmate Death with him.

'Do you need pigeons?' I asked.

He snorted with self-importance and brushed past me.

'Black leeches, then?' I called cheerfully as he went upstairs.

Doctor Turnbull ignored me and disappeared into my stepmother's chamber.

'Do you think we should call in a barber?' I asked Danes, who was down in the kitchen making gingerbread with Joan.

'Why, my little sparrow?'

'So that he can cut Maud's hair and we can put two dead pigeons at her feet.'

Danes laughed. 'There is not much wrong with the mistress.'

'How do you know that?' I asked disappointedly.

'Because she eats enough for a small army, toothache or no toothache.'

'It would be better,' said Joan, 'if she fed her eyes a little more and her stomach a little less.'

At the end of the week my stepmother, still not having the strength to leave her chamber, called for the preacher.

'This is a good sign,' I said to Danes. 'Maybe now we should call the barber.'

Danes wrapped me in her arms. 'Little sparrow,' she said, 'there is no fairness in who lives and who dies. Death is one of the great riddles that none of us understand. Nothing, short of fire or plague, is going to do away with Maud Leggs. If there were pigeons, she would ask Joan to put them in a pie.'

There were some good things to be had from my stepmother being bedbound. We no longer had to say endless prayers each evening, and for the first time since the marriage I got to spend time with my father alone. Hester had to stay with her mother and so the two of us would eat together as in days gone by.

Then I would sit with him in his study while he went through his books.

I liked his study. It was the only chamber now untouched by Maud's hand, because my father kept it locked. He had moved things in here from other parts of the house, things he did not want Maud snooping into. Among them was my mother's oak chest that used to be in their bedchamber. It was very big with a heavy lid and was beautifully carved with hunting scenes and castles.

'What is in there?' I asked.

'All your mother's dresses,' said my father, opening it up. There on the top were the two miniature portraits that he had had painted when they were just married, and beside them the little casket I knew held my mother's fairy shadow.

It was like looking at treasure from a long lost world. Here, in amongst the fine silks, lay memories more precious to me than fairy gold. Once more I was haunted by the image of a ship drifting out to sea, and this time I could hear my mother's voice softly calling to me.

10

Bad News

*T*hree days later Maud was up from her sickbed, with a look of iron in her eyes.

'Good husband,' she said that evening when we were all seated for dinner, my father as silent as ever and Hester looking pale and troubled. 'I have gathered much strength from my prayers under the kind and learned counsel of the preacher Arise Fell, and it came to me that Coriander and my humble daughter would also benefit from his great wisdom in all matters concerning the Bible. If —'

She was interrupted by my father's steward, who came in and handed him a letter. As he read it, the colour drained from his face.

Maud continued, 'It would perhaps be to our advantage if Master Arise Fell were to live and board with us.'

'This cannot be so,' said my father, taking no notice of what she was saying. 'There must be a mistake.' He turned to his steward. 'Is the messenger still here?'

'He waits in the hall, sir, for your reply.'

'Oh Lord,' said my father, 'what more troubles wilt Thou heap on me?'

'Good husband,' said Maud, 'it is a sin to use the Lord's name in vain. Blasphemy is a hanging offence.'

My father stared at her astonished, as if she were of feeble mind.

'We should be praising the good Lord and thanking Him for providing food for us to eat,' said Maud, stuffing another large piece of meat into the tiny slit of her mouth.

'No, woman,' said my father so sharply that even Maud looked taken aback. 'I have provided this food and all the other comforts of this house, and I advise you to start praying that this table will still have food upon it tomorrow.'

'What do you mean?' said Maud, nearly choking. 'Good husband, is all well?'

'No and no again,' said my father, getting up from the table, 'all is not well.'

'Then all I can say is, the Lord be praised for sending us a preacher who can guide us through these troubled times.'

'Mistress, what are you blabbering about?' said my father.

'Arise Fell,' said Maud. 'Were you not listening, good husband?'

My father walked towards the door. 'Oh Lord, give me strength,' he said.

'I take it then that you have no objection,' said Maud.

The door groaned shut behind him. Whether he had said yes or no I could not tell. Maud just sat there, and, smiling, helped herself to more roast beef and refilled her glass of claret.

*L*ater I found my father in his study, sitting at his desk. I put my arms around his neck and rested my head on his back.

'I am to be arrested,' he said.

'Why?' I asked.

He hugged me tight. 'For helping King Charles escape, and for having used my ships to smuggle Catholics out to France. It will not concern you, my poppet. It will be sorted out swiftly.'

'When are they coming for you?' I asked. I was fighting back tears and a scream that sat like a flightless bird in my throat. I wanted to shout 'Do not leave me, please do not you leave me too.'

'Not yet,' said my father, 'though it is only a matter of time. The letter was from a well-wisher who wanted to warn me.'

The candle on his desk faltered, and we both looked up to see a crooked man standing in the doorway, his insect-green glasses shining back at us from the gloom of the hall before he disappeared.

The next day I was told by my father's apprentice Sam that his master had been called away on urgent business. I knew then that our fortunes had begun to ebb away like the sand in an upturned hourglass.

That morning, while I sat with Hester, I caught a glimpse of hell. Maud came into my chamber, followed by the crooked man. Far from being dismayed at what had befallen her husband, she looked as pleased with herself as ever I saw a person look.

'This,' she said with great pride, 'be the preacher.'

He was, I knew without a shadow of doubt, the same crooked man that I had seen outside Master Thankless's shop, the same man who had watched my father and me from the hall. He was dressed in black. Tight was his coat, shiny were the patches on his elbows and pockets, dirty was the white collar round his neck. His hair was thin and long, hanging down in rat-tails. The smell about him was of mildew and his green glasses caught the light. He was a cockroach of a man.

As he introduced himself I realised that he was no stranger to Hester. She did not look at him but kept her eyes on the floor, and I could sense every muscle in her body tighten.

'I am Arise Fell,' said the preacher. 'My name speaks my purpose, to raise you out of your wickedness so that you may never fall into sin again.' He put his hands together in prayer and continued, 'Arise, O Lord, save them, for God is our light and our salvation.'

I felt a shiver go down my back, as I had done when I first saw him that day on the bridge.

Then, looking straight at me, he said, 'Ann, daughter of Eve, come here.'

I wondered to whom he was speaking and turned to look round the room in case anyone had come in while he had been preaching at us. Hester gave me a nudge. Slowly and uncertainly I went forward.

'Ann, what do you see?' he asked, holding his thin empty hands out towards me. He had dirty fingers and a long yellow thumbnail that curled over like the claw of a bird.

'Nothing,' I said.

He turned his hand palm up.

'What do you see now?'

'Still nothing,' I said, puzzled.

'In this hand,' said Arise, slowly advancing his empty right palm, 'is the wrath of God. In the other is His salvation. Now tell me again, what is your name?'

'Coriander Hobie,' I replied.

A cruel smile curled the corner of his mouth and he slapped me hard across the face. I was so startled that I stood my ground, unsure as to whether it had really happened.

'I will ask you again. What is your name?'

'Cor-i-an-der,' I said very slowly, and this time he hit me so powerfully that I found myself halfway across the floor.

'Leave her,' said Arise as Hester bent to help me. 'Get up,' he commanded, towering crookedly above me. 'Get up now.'

He grabbed me by my jacket and dragged me up to my room, his long thumbnail jabbing into the back of my neck. He pushed me into my chamber and locked the door.

I sat on my bed feeling bewildered and angry, certain that at any minute my father and Danes would come and rescue me and have the crooked man thrown from the house. I waited as the hours ticked mournfully past.

At last the key turned in the door and Danes stood there. I rushed to her and threw my arms about her.

'I am sorry, my little sparrow,' she said. 'It has taken me the best part of the morning to find the key. He had it hidden.'

'Where is my father?'

'I wish I knew,' said Danes. 'He told me there was a warrant out for his arrest for helping the King escape. He is in a lot of trouble, that much I know.'

'I just want him to come back and tell the crooked man to leave.' Tears of rage were rolling down my face. 'What right has he to be here?'

'Shush, my little one, shush,' she whispered, and she took me down to the kitchen where I was given ale to drink and the rest of a turkey pie to eat.

I stayed by the kitchen fire with Danes most of that afternoon. At last Arise walked in, my stepmother following behind like a small round pig.

'What is the meaning of this?' he said. 'I thought I had made it quite clear that this child was to stay in her room until all sinful vanity had fallen from her.'

'You have no right to give orders in this house, sir,' said Danes, standing up straight. 'When Master Hobie returns I will tell him how you conduct your lessons.'

'You will not be seeing Master Hobie again,' said Arise calmly. 'He is to be arrested for plotting against our great and mighty Lord Protector, Moses himself. He has been aiding and abetting the sinners from Babylon, smuggling them out of the country, helping the son of the Devil to escape these shores.'

'You have no right to speak of my father so,' I shouted. 'This is not your house.'

'Silence, child, or the hand of wrath will find thee,' said Arise.

'How dare you,' said Danes. 'The Lord said suffer the little children —'

'Oh, I have,' interrupted Maud, 'I have suffered them much, I have.'

'Do you know what is written here, Mistress Mary Danes?' said Arise, shaking a bundle of papers he was holding.

'No, how could I, sir?' said Danes. 'I cannot read.'

'Here is an indictment against you,' he said, 'an indictment from God-fearing honest people who have witnessed what has been going on in this house and will stand up and say so in court if needs be.'

'That's right, Arise. You tell the witch,' said Maud, rubbing her hands together.

Arise carried on like a preacher in the pulpit. 'It says in good, pure, upright letters that you have been seen hiding evidence relating to your late mistress's charms and remedies. That you have used Gabriel Appleby, the tailor's apprentice, to remove the remaining herbs and potions that bear witness to Satan's hand.'

He was fair shouting now. The house began to shake. He straightened himself as much as a crooked man can, and lightning seemed to flash from his glasses.

'Witches, fairy meddlers, sorcerers and all that seek their help sin against the commandments of the Lord. I believe, O God be my witness, that you, Mary Danes,' and he jabbed his long finger towards her as if it were a knife, 'are in league with the Devil and all his cohorts.'

'Oh,' said my stepmother admiringly, 'you speak so lovely.'

'I have done nothing wrong,' declared Danes.

'Let that be for others to judge,' shouted Arise. 'I believe the authorities will be much interested in what is written here.'

Danes was quiet and I felt my world crumble as Arise said menacingly, 'I have enough evidence to have you thrown into the clink, woman. As for your precious master, why, a hangman's noose waits for him at Tyburn. Who then will care for this miserable child?'

Hester let out a gulp. I ran to Danes and clung tight to her. She was my anchor, all that was left of the sinking ship.

'Do I make myself understood? If you want to keep your position here, you will think carefully before you interfere with my teachings again.'

I clung to Danes all the tighter, but Arise grabbed me and once more dragged me upstairs and shut me in my chamber.

That night I lay in bed in my gold-painted room and wept until Beth's face was soaked with tears. I watched the reflections of the river water dance on the walls and took comfort from the sounds outside. Our world might be lost but things were going on as usual, watermen arguing over passengers, drunks shouting their love to the moon, cats screaming their fury, the night watchman marking the hour.

Around first light my chamber door opened and my father crept in and sat on my bed.

'Shush, poppet, listen to me carefully,' he said. 'No one knows I am here. I have come to say goodbye. I must go away, I know not for how long, but all will be lost if I stay.'

'Take me with you then,' I begged. 'Please.'

'I cannot, my princess. It is not safe.'

'It is not safe here,' I said.

My father smiled and wiped away my tears. 'It is safer than where I am bound.'

'Please, I will be good, I promise,' I said, clinging to him like a drowning sailor.

'Coriander, I will come home to you. Just be brave for me. I do not do this lightly. Danes will look after you. But now I must leave, the barge is waiting.' He kissed me and I finally let go.

I watched from my window, tears blurring my vision as in the dull morning light I saw my father's barge make its way downriver towards Deptford.

I am not sure what hour it was when Arise Fell came into the room, this time with a servant carrying buckets of water and brushes.

I backed into a corner in fear of the wrath of God.

'These walls,' said Arise, 'are to be scrubbed until all these images of vanity, these scribblings of the Devil are gone. Do you understand?'

It took a week to wash away those pictures. I did it more with tears than water until only a faint outline remained, and as each wall was washed clean I put the story into my memory.

On the seventh day the crooked man came up the stairs with my stepmother behind him.

'What is your name?' asked Arise Fell.

'Ann,' I replied.

'Amen,' said my stepmother.

I knew then that my name had been stolen from me and locked away in the study. I would have to find it, for without my name who was I?

11

Farewells

Ships need good anchors, for without them they start to drift out to sea. So it was with our house. One by one the servants sadly shook their heads and left, until soon only Danes and Joan remained. In truth, poor Joan was too frightened to be of much use to us. Maud and Arise put the fear of the Lord into her, calling her a thief and accusing her of taking meat and other victuals. Arise threatened to have her thrown into Newgate Jail, which was as good as a death sentence. Joan went as white as a plucked chicken and started trying to cook her way to salvation. Now my only security was my beloved Danes, and my fear of losing her was great.

In the early days after my father's departure I pinned my hopes on Master Bedwell coming to our rescue. It was not to be. Under the watchful eye of Arise Fell, Maud Leggs (as I thought of her) became well versed in what to say to visitors like Master and Mistress Bedwell when they came to enquire how we were all doing in these troublesome times. For not only was there a warrant for my father's arrest but three of his ships had been reported lost at sea. Master Bedwell offered his help.

Maud held a cloth to her nose and said, 'Oh, I thank you for your concern. It has all been such a terrible blow. My dear good husband has, I am certain, been wrongly accused and is doing what he can to save his name and business. To that end he has gone away. I pray daily for news from him.'

Then she squeezed out a tear, and flapping her hand up and down like a fan whispered, 'Tell me, Master Bedwell, that it be not true what they say about my good husband having been a Royalist supporter.'

All this was said while Hester and I stood by her chair, our heads bowed, our eyes kept firmly on the floor.

Master Bedwell looked mighty uncomfortable and said that as far as he knew Thomas Hobie was a good and honest gentleman.

'My thoughts too,' said Maud, dabbing at her eyes. 'And all this talk of helping Papists is no more than lies.'

Patience kindly asked after me.

'As you can see, Ann is well,' replied Maud.

'Do you mean Coriander?' said Patience.

'Indeed I do not,' said Maud Leggs. 'We call her Ann to bring her back to the ways of the Lord. It is not good for a child to be indulged with a name that invites vanity. Ann be a good Christian name.'

Patience looked worried and at a loss as to what to say.

Oh yes, Maud Leggs and Arise Fell knew how to stifle criticism. As the visitors turned to leave, Maud said, 'I thank you so much for your concern. Do come again. Our gates are always open to honest godly folk.'

Arise led them out into the hall and said piously, 'I am praying daily for Master Hobie's safe return, just as I pray daily that the Lord Jesus Christ will soon see fit to come to London and take up his crown.'

The Bedwells never came again to enquire how we were faring.

To the good mistresses of Arise Fell's flock, who rushed to our house clucking like hens to peck their mean beaks into our affairs, to them Maud Leggs would say, weeping into her cloth, 'If I had known that my husband was a Royalist supporter, I would never have married him.'

'Indeed not,' the Bible-clutching ladies would say as they ate our sweetmeats and drank my father's fine wines.

'And when I think,' sniffed Maud, 'that my first husband (God rest his soul) was a hero who fought with Cromwell at the Battle of Naseby and laid down his life for the great cause! He must be turning in his grave.'

Cluck, cluck, cluck, went the good mistresses.

'This be my daughter,' said Maud, pointing at Hester. 'And that be my husband's child. If it were not that I should care for her I would have left this city and returned home long ago.'

With that the clucking ladies bobbed off home to spread the gossip like grain in a hen coop.

Now no one came to ask how we were faring or when my father might be expected back. I was no better than a prisoner in my own home. I slept alone in the kitchen, getting up early every day and not resting until late at night. I was nothing more than a maid of all work. Anyone who saw me would have found it hard to believe that once I had been the merchant's daughter who had a room painted with fairy stories and who wore dresses a princess might have owned.

By the time midwinter arrived, I had, through the drudgery of my days, lost all care as to what month it was, or even what year. Christmas came and went almost unnoticed, for Cromwell had banned the whole joyous Christmas festival.

Gone, all gone. Gone all the laughter, gone all the warmth. Now all that lingered in the dark nooks and crannies of the house were devils and demons, waiting to swallow me up.

All that was left of my old world was Beth, my beloved doll.

12

The Hand of Wrath

*N*ever in my life had I been as frightened of anyone as the crooked man. The sound of his footsteps on the creaking stairs was enough to fill my whole being with dread. When he hit me, I lost control and felt piss trickle down my legs, and I felt more ashamed of myself than any words can describe. He would look at me with disgust and say I was no better than a farm animal.

This crushed me. Hester never wet the floor, not even when her mother and Arise both went at her. Hester told me kindly that she was used to it. She had never known it any other way.

I hate to think what I would have done without Hester. She smuggled extra food to me and gave me blankets to keep me warm at night. She risked a good beating for her trouble if caught. Joan was too scared to give away a morsel of food and poor Danes was powerless to do more than offer words of comfort, though I could see it pained her not to be able to help me. In truth, I was so worried that she would be thrown

94

out that I begged her to say nothing, for she had no rights over our new lord and master Arise Fell.

One cold crisp morning after I had taken the coal up to the parlour, I stood on the landing gazing out of the window. It was snowing gently and the Thames once more looked like a scene from a fairy story, with all the houses and boats shining powdery white in the watery winter light. I wondered whether, if Lord Jesus did come, he would walk on water up the river to Whitehall, and whether the tides would stay still for him. Or would he ride on a donkey across London Bridge, and if so would he be able to see into all the houses and would he know about all the children who lived in fear of what was being done to them in his Father's name?

So lost in thought was I that I did not hear the crooked man creep up behind me.

'Vanity, all is vanity,' Arise breathed down the back of my neck. 'Idleness and vanity. You, Ann, were looking at your reflection and thinking yourself to be pretty, were you not?'

'No,' I said. 'I was not, sir.'

'Then what were you doing?'

'I was wondering when Jesus was coming.'

'How dare you use the Lord's name as an excuse!' shouted Arise. The hand of wrath once more found me and he hit me hard about the head so that my cap came undone and fell off.

'It is the Devil's work and no mistake,' he said, pulling hard at my hair. 'All these curls, red as the flames of Satan! This is vanity, this is pride.'

'What is going on?' said Maud, coming out of the parlour with Hester and peering up at us over the banisters.

'Nothing,' said Arise, dragging me down the steep steps to the kitchen. Bump. Bang. Bump.

'Where are the scissors?' he bellowed at a startled Danes and Joan.

'I do not rightly know where they are, sir,' said Danes.

Arise shook the dresser until plates and glasses fell off and the drawers slid open one after another, all crashing to the floor. Finally he found what he was looking for. All this time he gripped my hair tight.

'Leave her be,' said Danes shakily. I believe she thought he was about to kill me.

'Silence, woman. I did not ask for any of your tongue.'

He started to chop my hair off in handfuls. I did not fight back. What did any of it matter any more?

'How dare you!' said Danes, rushing forward. Arise pushed her away so that she lost her footing and tripped. She stood up again and said, 'How can you call yourself a man of God?'

Arise roared, 'Another word from you, mistress, and you will be thrown from this house. Do I make myself clear?'

Joan was whimpering. For the first time I was not crying. I looked on the floor with horror. For there, amongst all the broken plates, glasses, jugs, candles, pots and pans lay my beloved Beth. I had kept her hidden in the dresser for safety.

The sight of my doll made Arise stop chopping at my hair.

He let me go, and kicking a broken plate out of the way picked up Beth.

'Is this yours?' he said to me.

'Yes,' I said, feeling my legs go weak. 'May I have it, sir, please?'

'Is this doll cherished? Is this doll loved? To show regard for any image that is not that of the Lord is a sin,' spat out Arise.

'What harm is there in the child having a doll, when she has lost so much?' said Danes.

'This child,' said Arise, grabbing at me once more and shaking me hard, 'this wicked child has brought sin upon herself and she shall be punished.'

With a flick of his wrist he tossed Beth into the fire. I watched silently as my best beloved doll lay on top of the burning coals. Then the strangest thing happened. Beth stood upright in the fire with her cloth hands outstretched before her, and the flames, instead of going up the chimney, danced from the hearth towards the crooked man, like the forked tongue of a snake. Maud screamed with alarm as Arise's coat caught light so that he was forced to use the hand of wrath and the hand of salvation to beat out the flames instead of beating me.

A smell of singed wool filled the air, and still Beth stood there like Joan of Arc, refusing to be defeated by the flames. At last she dissolved into a myriad sparkling colours that fizzed and spat out from the fire, flying towards Arise and Maud who were forced to the end of the kitchen.

Arise, now white with rage, the veins in his forehead nearly bursting with anger, brought his fist down hard on upon the table.

'The Lord be my witness,' he shouted, pointing his long finger at Danes, 'this is proof of witchcraft for which I hold you, mistress, responsible. I order you to leave this house and never darken this door again.'

I ran to Danes and she took my hand. 'Let us be gone, my little sparrow.'

'No, you do not, you witch,' said Arise, suddenly grabbing me away from her.

'I will leave, sir, but let me take the child.'

'No,' said Arise coldly. 'Out, before I turn you over to the authorities, and may you have the grace to see the salvation that is offered you. The Lord is merciful.'

There was nothing else to be done. Danes was without any power. I knew that. I watched her go and felt all to be lost.

'Mother,' said Hester timidly.

'Silence,' hissed Arise. 'Joan, what are you staring and shaking for? Get on with the meal. And Hester, fetch a broom and clean all this up.'

I made one last desperate attempt to break free from the crooked man, determined that I was going to escape and run away with Danes, but he grabbed at me and dragged me to the study, followed by Maud. How he had got hold of the key to the room my father kept locked, I had no idea.

My mother's chest stood empty in the middle of the room with its lid open. Her dresses lay on the floor like lifeless butterflies. The little paintings were gone, the casket gone.

I knew then what the crooked man was going to do and the fear of it made me fight for my life. Finally I sank my teeth into his arm. He let out a yelp of pain and hit me so hard that I have no memory of being put in the chest, only of seeing the light disappearing.

I tried to push the lid open, but it was locked tight. I shouted for help but I knew no one would come. So I closed my eyes, for the darkness in my head was not as black or thick as the darkness I could see when my eyes were open.

This was it, then. I would become no more than a crumpled empty dress. Only my bones would be left to sing the truth of my death.

And so the second part of my tale is told, and with it another candle goes out.

PART THREE

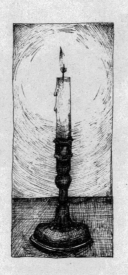

13

Medlar

I had always believed that there was only one world, the world I had been born into. Now I know that the world we live in is nothing more than a mirror that reflects another world below its silvery surface, a land where time is but a small and unimportant thing, stripped of all its power. For me it was my salvation, for without it I would be no more than dead bones in an oak chest in a grand house that once belonged to a London merchant.

I was certain that my end was near, that death was waiting for me. Terrified, I made one last desperate effort to push the lid open. It was hopeless, and I felt the darkness beginning to smother me.

Then there was light, wonderful light, blinding light, like the curtains being drawn back at a playhouse. I feared that I must be dead, for winter had melted away and here was summer as bright as Bartholomew Fair, with trumpets blazing, drums beating, and a chorus of crickets and birdsong to greet me. Wild flowers giddy in their scented finery and cow parsley as pretty as lace nodded in the breeze; hedgerows beckoned like market stalls full of fresh blackberries, and ripe strawberries giggled in their red gowns. The sky was blue, without a cloud to trouble it.

I turned round with a start to see a strange-looking man standing there. He had a long beard tied into a knot, and was holding a lantern as round as the moon. As surprising as he appeared, still there was something familiar about him, which rattled me, for I knew I had never met this man before.

'Wondrous fair!' he said, giving a deep bow. 'I was beginning to think you would not come. What took you so long?'

Was he talking to me? In truth, I was not sure, though there was no one else around.

'Am I dead?' I asked, which seemed to send the strange fellow into a fit of giggles, and he said, as if it were the funniest idea ever laid before him, 'Death and time do not belong here, Coriander.'

'How do you know my name? How did you know I would be here?' I stared at him, dumbfounded, and he held out his hand.

'Forgive me. I have not introduced myself. Medlar is the name I go by. I knew your mother when she was the same age as you, and was fortunate enough to meet your father one midsummer's night. A true gentleman, if I may say so.'

I stared at him, hardly even daring to whisper to myself what I thought. I felt that I was walking on water, so uncertain was I of everything, and that at any moment I would sink, be lost for ever below its shining ripples. For if a season can change in the closing of a chest, then maybe if I asked a question Medlar might vanish. So I kept quiet and accepted with joy that I was still alive, and took comfort in the knowledge that he had known my mother and had met my father.

'Ah, wondrous fair,' said Medlar again, as a horse and cart came plodding down the lane. I could hear a tinkling of bells and the sound of passengers singing merrily.

The driver stopped when he reached us and Medlar helped me up on to a seat.

The folk in the cart must, I thought, be going to a wedding, though no kind of wedding I had ever seen, for they wore skirts and petticoats, doublets and waistcoats, the like of which not even a Royalist would dare to put on. All had the most perfect shoes and none of them looked as if their bones might ache or their teeth be black or their hearts sad like the people of London. 'Welcome,' they said as they moved up to make room for us.

I sat there pleased that no one had asked Medlar what he was doing with such a ragamuffin. I felt out of place and was glad that no notice was taken of me whatsoever.

The cart jogged along and the passengers began to talk amongst themselves. I only half heard what they were saying; I was still perplexed as to how I could have come from cold darkness to such a brilliant summer's day. This is truly magic, I thought happily to myself.

'Knocked the milking stool away and down she went, legs

out in front of her,' laughed a lady sitting next to me. She was wearing a coat that looked as if it were made of thistledown.

'They ask for it,' said her friend.

'Indeed they do. Always wishing for this and that, never really knowing what it is they want. Then, when their wishes come true, instead of being happy, blow me down if they don't go wishing for something else,' said my neighbour.

'Exactly,' agreed the other one, 'never satisfied.'

'It is sad, though,' said the woman in the thistledown coat.

'True, but it brightens the day,' said her friend. And at that they both set off again in gales of giggles.

'Are you going to the wedding?' asked a gentleman with a large flower in his buttonhole.

'Of course,' answered Medlar. 'Where else would I be going on a midsummer's day like this?'

The gentleman leant forward in his seat. 'They say this marriage is all Queen Rosmore's idea.'

'So I have heard,' replied Medlar.

'It is wrong, I tell you,' said the man. 'It is like expecting fire and water to live happily together. We all know what happened last time they tried to force such a marriage.'

All the passengers nodded wisely.

I wanted to ask what had happened, but I felt shy. A man in a very tall hat who was sitting opposite us looked about him and then, lowering his voice, said, 'They say that if Prince Tycho will not marry Princess Unwin, the Queen will change him into a fox.'

'No! How terrible,' said the lady in the thistledown coat.

'There is a rumour that the Queen has the shadow already,' the man added with great importance, puffing out his chest like a chicken on a Sunday.

'You don't say!' said the lady.

'I have heard she is desperate to get that daughter of hers married,' said a stout lady carrying a cloth-covered birdcage. 'It is a great sadness they picked such a sweet prince, though. I do not know what he did to deserve this dubious honour.'

'I tell you this for nothing,' said the man in the tall hat. 'We shall all be lost if the Queen becomes any more powerful.' He crossed his arms and as he did so his hat flew from his head and tumbled down the lane like a drunken acrobat. The driver halted while he clambered out to retrieve it.

'No more rumours,' said the stout lady when he clambered back in. 'Today is the wedding. Let us wish the couple well and speak of happier things.'

I asked the stout lady what she had in the cage, but she just smiled sweetly and did not reply. I wondered if she might be deaf.

'What is in the cage?' Medlar repeated.

'Why,' she said straight away, 'a wedding gift, of course.'

She pulled off the linen and there, to my amazement, was a golden bird that began to sing. The bars of the cage were twisted like barley sugar and as I gazed at the bird, they glowed with a reflected blue light that leapt and danced in the sunshine.

'Oh, mighty fine,' I cried.

'It is for the bride.' She looked at it uncertainly. 'Do you think she will like it?'

'Of course she will,' said Medlar kindly.

The cart clip-clopped on its way until we came to a fork in the road. Ahead of us was the same grassy lane that we had been travelling down. To the left was a road that ended before it began in a tangle of brambles and briar roses. Yet it was to this road, where the thorns glittered like iron teeth, that the driver turned his cart. I hardly dared look, sure that we were going to be torn to pieces. Instead the brambles and briars parted for us as if they had been waiting for our arrival. Then, once we were safely through, they fell back amongst themselves like thieves into a quarrel.

Medlar smiled at me. 'Not far to go now,' he said.

We journeyed on up a drive until we came to some large wrought-iron gates that opened for us and then closed again without the help of human hand. I looked round at my fellow passengers, waiting for some sort of comment, but they took no notice, as if coming through brambles and iron gates that opened and closed for you was something that happened all the time.

On we went, clattering over the gravel until we came to a bend in the drive. Before us stood the most magnificent house I had ever seen, with windows that went right down to the ground and columns of marble that shone like pearls. Was it possible for a house to have so much glass and all of it to shimmer and shine as if the sun himself was playing host to the wedding? It was, alas, only a glimpse. The cart drove on and the house vanished again behind a screen of silver birch trees. I longed to see more, I longed to go inside, I longed for the cart to stop.

14
The Blue Light

We came to rest in a stable courtyard. Here there was more commotion than on London Bridge on market day, for every square inch of space was taken up with carriages and coaches, some, like ours, no more than country carts, others so fine that they must have belonged to kings and princes.

We climbed out, pleased to stretch our legs. Our fellow travellers straightened their hats and dusted down their skirts, all talking at once. They said their farewells to Medlar and promised to look out for him.

'Who lives here?' I asked when they had gone.

'This is the summer palace of King Nablus and Queen Rosmore. Tomorrow Rosmore's daughter Unwin is to be married.'

'Is that good?' I asked.

Medlar laughed. 'Good for the Queen and her daughter, bad for the bridegroom. He is being forced into this marriage against his will.'

'He should stand his ground.'

Medlar smiled. 'There are times when it is wiser to give in and survive than risk the wrath of the Queen.'

I wanted to know more and I had a thousand questions to ask him, but we were interrupted by a jester with a white face. He was wearing a cap tied neatly in a bow under his chin and had a ruff as fancy as that of Sir Walter Raleigh.

'I am so glad to have found you,' he said. 'My old friend, where have you been? I have something so exciting to tell you. Come this way and I will show you.'

Medlar turned to me. 'I am sorry,' he said. 'I must go. Do not worry; you will be all right. I will come and fetch you later.'

'Wait!' I cried. 'Let me come with you!'

But Medlar and the jester had disappeared into the crowd. Fearful of being left behind altogether, I ran after the wedding guests. In the hazy sunshine they looked like brilliant butterflies, fluttering and dancing their way into the great house. I stood there wondering if I dared follow them.

The hall was as cool as a stream after the warmth of the sun and my eyes took a moment to adjust to the light. It was very beautiful and spacious, with a vast marble staircase that swept up to a gallery from which wedding guests looked down on the new arrivals. I felt terrified, sure that I must stand out like a burnt tree after a thunderstorm.

Footmen were wandering around with silver salvers, offering tall goblets of wine. Anxious not to be asked to leave, I went off in search of somewhere to hide. There were several rooms to choose from. One had a table laid for the wedding feast, another had panelled walls and an enormous fireplace. Most were full of people milling around.

Eventually I found a long, elegant room hung with great gilded mirrors. Spindly gold chairs lined the walls and the wooden floor shone like honey. Never in all my life had I seen so much looking-glass. I walked up and down the room staring in all the mirrors. I could not make head nor tail of it, for I could not see my reflection anywhere. The mirrors showed quite clearly a room that went on and on, with endless gilt chairs waiting for endless ladies and gentlemen to rest upon them. But I, Coriander, was not there. There was just a blue light that moved when I moved and stopped when I stopped. I thought the mirrors must be made of magic glass that thought little of the vanity of man.

Just then a group of children came noisily in, taking off their shoes to slide on the polished floor. I looked in the mirrors and much to my puzzlement saw their reflections. Like the chairs, like the room, there they were. Why was I not there too?

I was much surprised as they started running straight towards me. I moved quickly out of the way and still they came on. I ducked this way and that, but it made no difference. I slipped behind the chairs and watched, as for a moment the children, perplexed, stopped their chase. I eased myself out and once again they started their game. I discovered that if I faced them they ran for me, if I turned away they stopped.

I put my hand up to my head.

'It has gone,' said a small boy, disappointed.

'No, there it is,' said another as I took my hand away. I did it again and again. The tiny blue light appeared. The tiny blue light disappeared. I felt excited, for if all that could be seen of me was a tiny blue light, then I could be bold.

I left the children and went out into the hall with a braver heart. I climbed the stairs, weaving in and out of the crowd, and sat in the gallery at the top, as I had done so often in our London house, to watch the guests arrive.

Here the ladies and gentlemen minded not how brilliant they appeared, feared not the laughter of others. They were as glorious in their colours as peacocks and parrots, as delicate as dragonflies and moths. There were gowns made of rose petals, jewels fashioned from dewdrops, silks so fine they could have been woven by spiders. What my father would not have given to buy such fabrics!

Since my mother's death, my world had slowly tumbled and crumbled down around me, all the joy and colour rinsed from it. Arise had near defeated me with his hand of wrath. The tiny blue light had all but blown out. Yet here in this exotic world, amongst these fantastical people, I felt that I had truly come home and that the blue light could begin to dance in joy amongst the wedding guests, for here was my salvation.

My happy thoughts were interrupted by loud voices from one of the corridors that led off the gallery. I started along it but then, afraid of getting lost, I turned to make my way back again. Suddenly I heard a sharp crowing sound, and looked up to see a huge black feathery cloak of a bird flying towards me. Frightened, I bent down low as it passed. It was a monstrous raven, its outstretched wings brushing the sides of the wide corridor. It flew right up to the double doors at the end, which immediately opened as if waiting for its arrival.

I followed without thinking what I was doing or what danger I might be in, and found myself in a panelled bedchamber, the walls and ceiling painted with fairy stories, very like my room back at home. In the centre of it was a four-poster bed. Huge windows came down to the floor and looked out over the formal gardens. Sitting at a table at the other end of the chamber was a plump young woman. I had a feeling that this must be Unwin. I could see her reflection in the mirror, with double chins that spilled down on to her chest. She was dressed in stays, her flesh squeezing out like an over-filled meat pie.

The raven took no notice of her. Instead he hopped on to the arm of a wing-backed chair, the occupant of which I could not see.

'My beauty,' said a woman, her voice harsh, 'where have you been?'

I moved slowly back, fearful of floorboards creaking, and put a hand over my forehead in case my blue light could be seen. I wished I had not been so hasty in following the raven into the room. Please, I thought, let him not speak. He must not talk. I did not want my fears to be confirmed.

'Is the prince here?' shouted the young woman.

'He is on his way, Your Highness,' replied the raven.

'Hasten, Unwin, make yourself ready,' said the figure in the chair.

'That dress does not become me,' whined Unwin as a waiting woman scurried into the room with a billowing cloud of white lace and satin. She started to pull at the dress so that the fabric ripped. The lady in the chair rang a bell and a chambermaid rushed into the room.

'I am not wearing it,' said the bride, stamping her foot. She lifted the powder puff she had been playing with and hit it down on the dressing table so hard that a cloud of powder went everywhere, choking the poor maid. 'Get out, you imbeciles,' she shrieked. 'See what you have done!'

The maids looked towards the wing-backed chair and I could see a long bird-like hand dismiss them. They curtsied and quickly made their escape.

The owner of the hand stood up tall and straight and walked over to the bride. I thought of the conversation on the cart. This then must be Queen Rosmore.

'Be calm, my darling daughter. Such worries are not worthy of you. Nothing will go wrong this time. Trust me. Cronus and I have everything arranged.'

I knew then with a sickening certainty that I had met the raven before and that the lovely face of the Queen was only a mask. Behind it was the old witch I had met on London Bridge.

Queen Rosmore turned away from her daughter. She looked straight in my direction and said softly to the raven, 'Make sure Medlar is kept away this time.'

15

The Fox Prince

I ran down the marble staircase and out on to the gravel drive, relieved to be away from the Queen and her raven. I stood there not sure where to go, watching more wedding guests arrive.

Oh, what was happening? I was in a world where I felt I belonged, yet I had no presence. I had been brought here by a strange man who said he knew my mother. I had to find him to ask one question at least: was it my mother's shadow they were talking about? I had a sinking feeling that I knew the answer.

I felt cross with myself. I should be braver. I should be bolder, I should be fearless. But I could not. I was too bewildered by what I had seen.

I made my way away from the drive and slipped behind some clipped bushes. From my hiding place, I could see a woodland path that flickered with the scattered gold of sunshine. I followed it until I heard a sound I knew and loved. It gurgled, it lapped, it ebbed and flowed. There, down steep banks hidden by trees and shrubs, was the opal green of a river.

What is it about water, I wonder, that it always calms me? Maybe it was growing up near the Thames. Seeing the river felt like being greeted by a long-lost friend and I felt a sudden pang for my home and all that I had lost.

I rushed and tumbled down through a thick clump of purple foxgloves until very near the bottom I stopped, seeing a flash of brilliant white. I stood still, sure my eyes were fooling me. There, standing at the water's edge, was a white stallion.

The stallion looked at me as if seeing me, nodded his head and drank at the clear water.

I edged my way forward. A little way off, I could see a young man. He walked up to the horse and buried his head in its neck. I took a step closer. A twig snapped under my foot and the horse started, all white, all glistening.

To my alarm, the young man drew his sword.

'Who's there?'

I had never been interested in boys and had no notion that I ever would, seeing being in love and loving as a great tangle in which you could lose your head as well as your heart. Yet standing there that afternoon looking at the young man, I could well see how such knots in life were made.

'Who's there?' he said again. 'I know you are there. Show yourself. I fear you not.'

I stayed as still as I could. I knew then that this was the bridegroom they were waiting for. He was not meant to marry Unwin, of that much I was sure. The man in the cart had been right when he said it was like fire and water.

He sat down on the ground, his head in his hands. The horse came up to him and nuzzled at his neck and the young man rested his mop of black hair against the snow-white mane.

Forgetting I was no more than a tiny blue light, I said, 'Please, I mean you no harm.'

'Who are you? Show yourself.'

'I cannot,' I said.

'Then you are not the Queen trying to trick me?'

'No,' I said, 'my name is Coriander.'

I walked up to him. I could see the blue light reflected back at me. He had dark brown eyes. I felt a shock go through me as with great gentleness he touched my face, feeling my eyes, my nose, my mouth, my ears, as a blind man would see through his fingers.

I thought not to say this, for it embarrasses me to remember. But such tenderness had been gone from my life for so long that tears rolled down my face.

He took me over to the great white horse. 'Do not be scared. He knew you were here long before I did.'

The horse raised his head and, trembling, I stroked his mane.

'Where did you come from?' the prince asked.

'I do not rightly know,' I said. 'I was locked in a chest and I thought I was going to die.'

'Medlar was sure you would come one day, when the time was right,' said the prince, smiling. 'It is good to meet you at last.'

'What is your name?' I asked.

'Tycho,' he said. 'My name is Tycho.'

Behind us a branch snapped and his face darkened, as if a cloud were going over the sun.

'Has anyone else seen you?' he said.

'No.'

'Does the Queen know you are here?'

'No.'

I did not want him to walk away. I felt safe when he was near me. 'Why marry against your will?' I asked him.

'I have no choice. If I do not, Rosmore will cast a spell on me. I shall be changed into a fox and hunted down and killed.'

I felt worried by what he had said. Surely that could not be right.

'My mother told me fairy stories where such enchantments happen, but I never thought –'

'She told you stories of this world,' he interrupted, 'and here there are such spells.'

'Why would the Queen want to be so cruel?'

He said nothing. Above us, the sky darkened and through the trees the raven, heavy with his inky black feathers, swooped down towards us. The horse reared. I drew back to hide in the undergrowth. The huge bird landed on a branch near Tycho.

'What keeps you from the house?' demanded Cronus.

'Nothing. I am thinking of what lies ahead.'

'All that fortune can bring,' crowed the bird, his pearl black eyes glittering. He pointed with the tip of his wing to a tower that rose above the forest. 'The Queen has been watching for you. She has sent huntsmen to escort you.'

I looked up to see giant riders approaching the bank. Their jackets were the colour of wet blood and their dogs barked and snarled, showing sets of teeth as sharp as knives. I felt pity for the horses. They were small, much too small for the riders, and their eyes were wild with fear, their ears pinned back as they stamped the ground.

Tycho walked over to his great white horse. It stood many hands taller than the huntsmen's terrified beasts, and looked majestic in the golden light. Tycho looked straight at me, and for a moment I thought I must be visible and blushed to think what he would make of me with my ragged dress and ill-cut hair. He touched my arm and whispered, 'I will not forget you. Do not forget me.'

I could see the raven looking in my direction and I knew that I must do something. I went close to Tycho and said as softly as I could, 'Do not go through with this marriage. Follow what your heart tells you.'

Tycho looked towards me for a moment and then turned to follow Cronus.

I felt unbearable sadness come over me as I watched the huntsmen and the dogs accompany the bridegroom and his horse up to the house. I thought that he looked as if he were about to be hanged at Tyburn.

16

Embroidered Eyes

I knew that I could not stay in hiding. I would have to find Medlar. Maybe he would be able to stop this wedding and save Tycho from his fate.

It was getting late by the time I arrived back at the house. The big black dog of night with its belly full of stars had already rolled over on the day.

In the entrance hall, everyone was gathered in great excitement. They whispered like a flock of birds at eventide before being ushered into the long chamber with the mirrors and the spindly gold chairs. The doors closed behind us with a loud, mournful clang. It sounded like a bell tolling for a funeral.

I stood at the end of the chamber hoping to catch sight of Medlar, but he did not appear. Where could he be? I did not know what to do. Should I go back to the stables?

By now everyone was seated and silent. Then trumpets sounded and the great doors opened once more to reveal Queen Rosmore, standing tall and proud in a gown that trailed behind her. At her neck was a ruff of fur and on her hair a black head-dress made of feathers, flightless and heavy. Her gown was covered in a hundred embroidered eyes that moved, opening and closing, staring out, searching for something or someone.

King Nablus entered behind her. He looked shaky and weak and was leaning on a stick, his body twisted like an ancient walnut tree, his long white hair hanging over his shoulders. He stood out amongst the wedding guests, carrying the weight of time on his shoulders. He nodded to the crowd, and as he approached the men bowed their heads, the women curtsied.

I moved along the great hall, staying close to the walls, pleased to see my blue light reflected back, dancing with all the other lights in the room. The King and Queen made their way to a dais. The King was helped into his chair by attendants and sat there awkwardly, his face frozen as if in surprise.

Tiny bells began to chime, rose petals fell like snow and little lights twinkled across the room. It was the setting for a perfect fairy tale wedding. Yet I knew, as did the guests, that something was very wrong.

The raven flew in and landed on the Queen's outstretched arm. She bent her head as he whispered something in her ear.

'Is there a stranger amongst us?' she asked suddenly.

The room was quiet. You could hear the rose petals falling, such was the silence.

I was sure I had been discovered. I felt a sound rise in my throat. My relief was enormous when I heard the guests cry with one voice, 'No strangers here.'

'Then let the wedding begin,' said the Queen.

The trumpets sounded and the hall was filled with music as the bride and groom came in. The bride, older than the prince, looked as if she was accompanying a wayward nephew to a dance, not a bridegroom to a marriage.

I was taken aback when I saw her dress. It was just like the one in the painting of my mother. Flowers were woven into her hair, too. The difference was that my mother had been beautiful and had loved my father. This bride was no beauty and loved no one so much as herself.

The music stopped and a trembling man came up on to the dais. He seemed terrified and was given more to starting sentences than finishing them. It was only when the Queen brought her gloved hand down hard on the arm of her chair and Cronus had flapped his black wings that he found his tongue.

'We are here today,' he stuttered, 'for the joining of a prince and princess in marriage. We are here to bear witness that this marriage takes place with a true heart and a free spirit –'

'Enough! Marry them and have done with it,' said the Queen.

The bridegroom stepped forward and addressed the Queen.

'I cannot do this,' said Tycho. The crowd gasped. 'Forgive me,' he went on, turning to the wedding guests. 'I cannot marry without love. I do not love the princess and I never will.'

'He is being foolish. He knows not what he is saying. Get on with it!' shouted the Queen.

'Get on with it,' screeched Unwin, pulling and pushing at

the trembling man so that he was unable to speak. 'Say the word and then he is mine.'

Tycho left the dais and started to walk away from her down the long room.

'Close the doors,' ordered the Queen, and they slammed shut with a sound of finality.

Her face was again calm, her expression all softness.

'Let us have no more of this childish behaviour. Tycho, come back and let the marriage continue.'

The King suddenly stood up and stumbled forward to the edge of the dais.

'A marriage? Is it my darling daughter? Is that my beloved?'

His attendants rushed to him and led him back to his seat.

'Let the King speak,' said Tycho. 'If you dare, let the King speak.'

The Queen looked wild with fury and the wedding guests hastily got up off their spindly gold chairs.

'No!' screamed the bride, her voice so high that the gilded mirrors shattered. 'I will not have my wedding ruined.'

In that instant green lightning came from the Queen's fingers and struck Tycho, who fell to the ground.

'I will finish you off myself,' she yelled. 'What need have I for huntsmen or shadows? I will have my way.'

'Do it then,' said Tycho, getting to his feet. 'Come on, do your worst.'

The Queen threw another bolt of green lightning and again he went down.

Gilt chairs fell to the floor. Men, women and children cowered in fright. Without thinking, I ran to where Tycho lay.

'Are you all right?'

'Yes,' he whispered, picking himself up. 'But you must get away from here. It is not safe.'

The Queen, seeing Tycho on his feet for the third time, said to the terrified guests, 'Come, everyone be seated. The wedding will take place as arranged.'

'There will be no wedding,' said Tycho. His voice rang out loud and clear.

The magnificent doors flew open. There was the great white horse. Even the Queen backed away when she saw him, and all the eyes on her gown closed.

Tycho kissed my cheek, mounted and was gone. With his departure the guests ran from the long room. I stayed where I was, frozen to the spot.

The Queen was standing over her daughter who lay on the floor, banging her fists and kicking.

'You promised,' shouted Unwin, 'you promised that nothing could go wrong. You said you would be all-powerful and everyone would have to obey you.'

'What is happening?' said the King. He stood up and, shaking pitifully, called again, 'Is that my daughter? Is that my beloved?'

The Queen looked in my direction. All the eyes on her gown now opened wide. 'Who is there?' she cried.

I turned to flee.

'I know who you are. I will find you. There is no hiding place. You will pay for this,' she hissed.

I ran from the room. The hall was now deserted, the gravel drive empty. When I looked back over my shoulder, all I could see was the moon reflected in the many windows of the house.

I ran, oh how I ran. I did not know where I was going but I did not stop until I reached a barn, and here I curled up exhausted in the straw and fell fast asleep.

17

The Lost Land

I woke astonished to find my hair once more long and thick about my head. I was in a carved ebony bed, the daylight playing at the curtains so that rays of sunshine cut through the sleepy darkness. A shaft of sunlight hit upon a basin of steaming water. I sat bolt upright. How could this be? Last night I had gone to sleep in a barn. Who, I wondered, had seen fit to carry me to this bed? I thought it must have been Medlar, and a deep sense of relief came over me.

I got out of bed. There were my clothes laid out, washed and mended as if someone had just come into the room and, having made all ready for my morning, had quietly left.

I got dressed and opened the door, sure I would find Medlar waiting.

I went out into the corridor and realised that I was still in the summer palace.

No, this could not be. At any moment the Queen might appear and find me. I went back into the bedchamber and closed the door. At first, what I saw made no sense. In the space between the opening and the shutting of a door, the bedchamber as I remembered it had changed completely, as if a spell had been cast over it.

Everything in the room was covered in a layer of thick dust. The curtains that the sun had been badgering were now no more than a mass of spiders' webs. The bedcovers were all torn and tattered, feathers spilt from the mattress, and the washbasin was cracked and broken as if long abandoned. It was a room of rags and feathers, nothing more.

My head ached as it does at the onset of a storm. I looked outside. The corridor too had been transformed. The fine Persian carpets that had lain on the polished floor were no more, replaced instead by dry leaves that rustled as I walked. The house groaned, its timbers creaking like a great galleon wrecked on the shore of neglect.

I stared up at the ceiling that when last I had looked had been painted with fairy tales. I could see a heavy, cold sky winking at me through a large hole in the rafters.

I listened, and hearing no human sound I decided to be brave and go downstairs to the room where the wedding was to have taken place.

The glass in the shattered mirrors had clouded over. The rain-soaked floor was strewn with faded petals and gilt chairs. I started as I heard a scraping noise and for one moment my hopes rose. Perhaps Medlar was here. I rushed up to the dais where two chairs still stood, now covered in moss. A spider crawled out from one of them. The great doors that had opened and closed on command hung swaying on their hinges like drunken men.

I went back into the hall. I no longer feared the Queen's arrival. I knew that this place was too long deserted. It was as if I had been asleep for a hundred years.

I ventured into another room. It was dark, the windows boarded over. Here I found a mighty oak table. The end nearest to me had upon it a fresh white tablecloth, pressed in a perfect square. A bowl full of hot porridge was waiting for someone to eat it. Next to it was a jug of warm creamy milk, a loaf of freshly cut bread, butter, and honey. At the centre of the cloth was a candle, the wick already trimmed.

I sat down and ate as if I had not eaten for months, so great was my hunger. At last, more than full, I sat back and watched as a beetle slowly made its way along the table.

I stood up. The silence of the empty room seemed suddenly filled with menace and I remembered the stuffed alligator in my father's study. How frightened I had been in that other time, in my other world.

With my heart thumping, I left the house as fast as I could. It was so cold outside that my teeth started to chatter, and it dawned on me as I looked around at the bare trees that not only had the house undergone a transformation but so had the season. In the space of a sleep, winter had sunk her frozen claws into the earth.

Snow started to fall as I made my way down the gravel drive, its uneven surface evidence of horses and carriages. I walked on towards the stables. They too were deserted.

'Is anybody here? Medlar?' I called.

My voice echoed round the empty yard, but only the wind and snow whispered their reply.

I sat on a step near the frozen horse trough and wondered what to do. My fingers were numb, my feet hurt with the cold, my breath left a ghostly imprint on the air.

'Wondrous fair!' said Medlar. 'I have been looking for you.'

I looked up. I was so cold that I felt neither pleased nor sad to see him. Everything in me was frozen. Medlar wrapped his cloak round my shoulders and took me up into a room above the stables. Here a fire was lit. The floorboards were bare and the only furnishing was a table and two chairs. I sat down.

'Where have you been?' I said. 'Why did you leave me?'

Medlar did not reply. Instead, he sat me by the fire and rubbed my hands together to get them warm.

'I have to take you back,' he said.

'Take me back? Where?' I asked.

'Back to your home, back to London.'

'No,' I said, pulling my hands away from his. 'If you do that it will be the end of me.'

'I can assure you it will not.' Medlar picked up a pan from the fire and poured out two glasses of a warm spicy drink that seemed to flow straight down into my feet and fingers. He lit his lantern and the light bobbed there, a small moon in the smoky room.

'Who are you?' I asked.

He smiled at me. 'Who am I?' he repeated to himself, stroking his beard. 'A good question, and one for which there must be an answer. I am many things. I am a traveller. I am the King's magician. I am the searcher of shadows. I was your mother's teacher, and many moons ago I met your father on the London road. I can answer only a fragment of your question but, alas, it will have to do.'

'It was you,' I said then, remembering my father's story about meeting a man who had been robbed.

'I liked your father,' said Medlar. 'He did not wish, like other mortals, for things to be better. He accepted his fate with grace, and still had the heart to care for others. It was I who brought your mother to the London road. I thought that love and fate would do the rest, and I was right.'

I must have been staring at him open-mouthed, for he said, 'Drink up, and you will feel better.'

I sipped and felt warmth once more flood over me.

'Why did you not help Tycho?'

'If I had done so, Rosmore would have known I was there and all would have come to naught. You had the power to help, and you did,' said Medlar.

'But I am just a blue light,' I said. 'I have no power.'

'There is much you do not understand,' said Medlar. 'I made sure you were a blue light, to protect you.' He sighed.

'Did your mother tell you anything of this world?'

'Nothing but fairy stories,' I said.

'Surely she must have told you something of her childhood,' said Medlar.

I shook my head. 'No.'

I could see my reply disappointed him. 'Ah well, there's a thing,' he said sadly, pulling at the knot in his beard.

I did not like the idea that I knew nothing of my mother's past, so I said, 'I did see her shadow.'

'You did?' said Medlar. 'Oh, wondrous fair! When?'

'A long time ago, just after she died. It was in an ebony casket in my father's study.'

'What did it look like?' asked Medlar, his eyes never leaving mine.

'It was silvery, like gossamer. I never saw it again.'

'The shadow must be found and returned,' said Medlar.

'I do not understand. Why do you want it?'

'Your mother's shadow was the cause of much rejoicing, for a shadow that holds the glory of everlasting light is a rare shadow indeed, and one with a power so great that it can be used to do great and terrible evil. I know that the Queen is searching for it, and if she were to find it she would become all-powerful. It is now unattached and vulnerable. It has fallen into the hands of mortals who have played with it for their own gain, and in doing so have let a chink of human time into our world. You have seen proof of it in our dear King, and now in his summer palace.'

My thoughts were in such a whirl, and there was so much I wanted to know, yet all I could think to ask was 'Will I see my mother again?'

'No,' said Medlar gravely. 'That cannot be. She chose to die in your world. We have no power over death there.'

He pulled his chair near me and took my hand. 'I must ask you to try and find the shadow.'

'Me? No!' I said, terrified. 'I am not brave, I am not bold, I am not fearless.'

'At the wedding,' said Medlar, 'I deliberately left you to your own devices. I wanted to find out how much of your mother is in you. You have the heart of a lion, Coriander. You are brave enough to go into the Queen's bedchamber, bold enough to stroke a white charger, fearless enough to save a prince.'

I sat there lost for words, trying to make sense of all that had befallen me. I still found it hard to believe that this strange land was where my mother came from. Why had she never told me about it? I wondered. Why had she chosen death rather than return here?

Medlar said nothing as he saw the tears roll down my face. He leant down, picked up a linen-wrapped package from under his chair, and handed it to me.

Inside it were the silver shoes.

So many strange things had happened, and this still seemed the strangest of them all. I stared at them. I had forgotten quite how beautiful and dainty they were. I held them up to the light of the candle, where they glittered like glass.

'Coriander, these shoes were made for you and you alone,' said Medlar. 'There is no way that they would not have found you. They were made to grow with you. Unbeknown to me, a spell was put on them. Your mother managed to undo part of it, but not all. Now you may have them back.'

I picked them up. They were as soft and as light as swans' feathers.

'Once you put them on,' said Medlar, 'you will be back in the chest.'

A hunting horn sounded. It tore at the silence outside, cutting it like a knife. We both rushed over to the window and pulled back the wooden shutters. It was dark outside; snow was still falling and the silver birch trees were outlined blue against the black background. Between them galloped the great white horse, a fox running beside him. I could see the outline of the huntsmen and their dogs.

I knew then that Queen Rosmore had done her worst. Tycho had become a fox.

I felt a sharp pain in my middle finger and saw that I must have pricked it on the shutters, for three drops of blood fell into the freshly fallen snow. Red rubies, I thought, on white velvet.

A cry of 'Tallyho!' rang out through the landscape.

'If I find the shadow, will Tycho be saved?' I asked.

Medlar nodded.

I put my toes into the shoes.

'Tell me one last thing before I go. What was the name of King Nablus's daughter?'

And he told me what my heart already knew.

'Eleanor.'

*A*nd so the third part of my tale is told, and with it another candle goes out.

PART FOUR

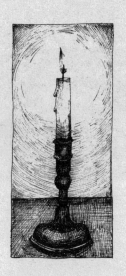

18

The Terrible Scream

I woke in utter darkness, curled up, unable to move. I knew myself to be back inside the chest. I could hear muffled voices and then a loud bang as the study door hit hard against the wall.

'No you don't! Out of my way, sir! This is an honourable God-fearing house. You have no right to come barging in here,' said the unmistakable voice of Arise Fell.

'If you do not let me in I shall call a constable. I have reason to believe that the body of Coriander Hobie is locked in a chest here,' said a gruff voice I did not know.

'Captain Bailey,' said a voice I recognised as that of Master Thankless, 'that must be the chest my apprentice talked about.'

Then I heard a small voice that sounded like Hester's.

'It be that chest, sir, she be locked in.'

'Quiet, you numskull. Keep that tongue from flapping in your head.' This was Maud.

'Open that chest immediately,' said the gruff voice.

'I shall not. It is not my chest and a preacher may not go into other men's property unless that property is offensive to the Lord.'

'I have heard that you have already got rid of many of Master Hobie's possessions. Now, open the chest.'

I knocked on the side of the chest with all my might. I must get out and find the shadow and save Tycho. There was no time to lose. I would have to explain all later.

'I am in here,' I shouted. 'Let me out!'

There was a terrible scream from Maud.

'Oddsfish! She is alive!' said Master Thankless.

'Hold on, we shall have you out in a minute,' said the gruff voice. 'Come, Master Thankless, let us find some tools. How could any man do such a thing? Call yourself a preacher!'

I heard the study door shut behind them.

I could hear Maud whimpering.

'Oooh, Arise, it is a ghost come back to haunt us! That girl's bones are going to sing and we shall be done for.'

'Quiet, keep your voice down, woman. Listen to me. We must keep to our story. She ran away. We thought she had gone off with Mistress Danes and drowned. Unbeknownst to us, by the use of witchcraft and devilry, she got back into the house and hid in the chest.'

'How then is it locked?' said Maud.

'Because the Good Lord saw fit to lock it.'

'Do you think it be her bones, Arise, that have been knocking in there?'

'No, woman, I do not.'

'I told you, you should have done what the lady asked while you had the chance,' said Maud. 'You should have tipped her body in the river and let the rats finish her off. If she was dead, we would have none of this trouble.'

'Be quiet, woman,' snapped Arise. 'You are no help. Let me think. We must keep our wits about us.'

'It is the Devil coming for us, Arise, and I can smell them gallows at Tyburn,' said Maud. 'You had better make those pretty words in the Bible work in our favour, for they will surely find putrid flesh and bones rotting in that chest.'

'Hold your feeble tongue. Let me do the talking.'

I heard people rush back into the room and with great urgency break open the lock and lift the lid.

For a moment, the light was so blinding that I could not see my rescuers. The room went very quiet. I stood up but I did not get out of the chest, for I was unsure of my feet.

Then I saw the familiar face of Master Thankless.

'Oh Master Thankless, I am so glad to see you!' I said.

'I am mighty pleased that you are alive,' said the tailor, 'and mighty puzzled by what has been going on here. Nothing adds up, no, it does not.'

'You do not know me, mistress,' said the gruff voice, 'but I am Captain Bailey. I sailed on one of your father's ships. A kinder and more honourable gentleman I have yet to meet.'

Then I remembered my father.

'Do you know where he is?' I asked.

141

'I know he is alive, but of his whereabouts I cannot tell you,' said Captain Bailey.

My eyes were now used to the light and I could see that the room, by some strange magic, had shrunk in size. So too had Maud, for if my eyes did not deceive me I was taller than she was. I was nearly as tall as Arise Fell and only a head shorter than the sea captain. How this could be I had no idea, though the effect of my appearance on everyone in the room was of complete disbelief. If it had not been for Hester I would have taken more note of their surprise, but the sight of her crumpled frame leaning against the wall gave me such a jolt that for a moment I was not even sure if it was she. She looked so thin and her eyes were hollow and her skin pale.

'I thought they had killed you,' sobbed Hester, 'and I could do nothing.'

'What have I told you, you half-witted girl! Quiet!' snapped Maud, raising a hand to slap her.

I got out of the chest. I looked at Hester and felt weighted down and tied back into this world. I knew I could not leave her like this.

The minute Maud saw me coming towards her she moved away and tried to hide behind Arise, who held his hands out in front of him. His voice wavered as he said, 'This is proof of witchcraft. You are surely the Devil's child.'

I bent down to Hester. She put her arms round my neck and said, 'I am so sorry I could not help you sooner. May God be my witness, I truly tried.'

Master Thankless gently helped Hester to stand. I could see it caused her pain.

'I do not know what has been going on in this house,' said Master Thankless, turning to Arise, 'but I can tell you that the only devil in this room, sir, is yourself. Come, Miss Coriander, you and Miss Hester are not staying here a moment longer.'

'I cannot, sir,' said Hester, feebly pulling her hand away. 'I am sorry, sir. I am sick. Best leave me here.' And she slid down the wall and sat slumped on the floor like my old doll Beth.

'Hester,' I said, 'what have they done to you?'

The sea captain picked her up as if she were no heavier than a bag of feathers. He turned to Arise. 'How can you call yourself a godly man?'

I followed Captain Bailey and Master Thankless out into the street where a carriage stood waiting.

When we were seated, Master Thankless looked at me with a mystified expression.

'Oddsfish, I can hardly believe my eyes, Coriander,' he said.

'How did you know where to find me?' I asked.

'My apprentice Gabriel Appleby has been keeping a watch on the house, and Hester found the courage to tell him,' said Master Thankless. 'But I can hardly fathom what has been happening here. By all the laws of nature you should be dead.'

He tucked a blanket about Hester and we rattled and rocked through Thames Street and up on to the bridge.

Outside the tailor's shop a young man was pacing up and down. All I could think was that Master Thankless had found himself another apprentice. I wondered why Gabriel was not there to meet us.

'You were not too late? She is not dead?' said the young man in much agitation as he helped Master Thankless lift Hester from the carriage.

'Not yet,' said Captain Bailey.

'Go, Gabriel, fetch the doctor,' said Master Thankless. 'Quick, lad.' And Gabriel ran off as if his life depended on it.

I watched him, bewildered. When I had last seen Gabriel he was but a lad, a little older than Hester, certainly not yet a man. I am like a sailor, I said to myself, one who has returned from a distant voyage, not knowing how long I have been gone, unsure of the season, uncertain of the year. I must have been looking lost, for Master Thankless took my arm and said kindly, 'Come, Coriander, help me get Hester inside.'

We got Hester up the stairs where Nell, the maid, helped me undress her. We were both shocked to see the whip marks on her back, as was the doctor when he came. He feared she might not make it through the night and said angrily that he would not treat his dog in such a manner and that London was full of charlatans and crooks who hid under the disguise of righteous men, preachers and prophets.

After the doctor had applied a poultice to Hester's bruises and given her some medicine, we washed her and put her to bed. I sat with her, holding her hand and trying in my head to make a straight line of all that had happened.

I must have fallen asleep for I woke with a start as if

someone had shaken me. I looked round and caught a glimpse of a face reflected in the window. For a moment I thought my mother was in the room and my heart started to beat faster. I was sure I could hear her voice telling me what to do. Then I realised that the face staring back at me was mine and mine alone.

I called for Gabriel to sit with Hester while I went downstairs, where I found Master Thankless and Captain Bailey deep in conversation.

'I have seen many strange things in my life,' the captain was saying, 'but by the saints' bells this is the strangest. If you ask me, there is some odd magic going on here.'

'Ah, Coriander,' said the tailor, seeing me, 'can I be of service?'

'I wondered if you still have my mother's remedies here.'

'Yes, indeed I have. They are kept safe in the cellar.'

'I believe there is one that could help Hester.'

'Then let me show them to you,' said Master Thankless, and he led me down the stairs.

The little bottles were packed in baskets with straw and all looked very much the same.

'This is a pickle and no mistake,' said Master Thankless. 'The bottles have no labels. There is no way of knowing what they are for, and Mistress Danes is not here to help us.'

'I must look for a bottle with a purple flower in it,' I said. 'I do not think Hester will live unless we find it.'

'I fear I have left this too late,' said the tailor. 'I should have gone to the house when Gabriel first told me how Hester was being treated. Well, you do one basket and I will do another. If there is such a bottle, we will find it.'

We carefully examined each bottle but it was no use. None of them had a purple flower in it.

I stood there at a loss. Then I thought that maybe the best thing was just to trust. I closed my eyes and picked out a bottle.

'If you are wrong,' said Master Thankless, trying to comfort me, 'I doubt it will make any difference.'

'Master!' shouted Gabriel. 'You should come! I think she's going.'

My heart was pounding as I rushed up the stairs, followed by Master Thankless.

Hester looked deathly white and she was making awful gurgling noises as she breathed. Captain Bailey said he had heard such sounds many times before from those who were about to meet their Maker.

Without a second thought I broke open the seal to the bottle and gently dripped the potion into her mouth, being careful not to spill a drop, just as I had seen my mother and Danes do. Then I sat holding one of Hester's hands while Gabriel held her other.

The moon had come to watch over her and shone in a pool of light on the bedroom floor. That night we all stayed with Hester and somewhere towards morning I remember falling asleep, to be woken by the cry of seagulls.

Gabriel too was asleep with his head resting on her bed, and Master Thankless was dozing in a chair by the door. Captain Bailey had left. He had told us that his ship was sailing on the morning tide.

Hester was breathing peacefully. As I let go of her hand to close the shutters she said faintly, 'Coriander?'

'Oh Hester,' I said, seeing her eyes open, and I burst into tears. 'You are still with us.'

'Where else would I be?' she said softly.

Gabriel, hearing her voice, raised his head.

'By the Good Lord, it is a miracle!' And he kissed her hand and was smiling and crying all at the same time.

As I watched Gabriel and Hester I thought indeed I must have been gone a long time, for when I left Hester did not even know Gabriel Appleby.

Master Thankless got up. He walked over to the table on which I had placed the empty bottle. He picked it up and held it towards the light.

'See, Coriander. There in it lies a purple flower.'

19

Stitches in Time

*U*p to that moment, I had tried to ignore the fact that something about me was different. However, in the slow days that followed Hester's recovery, it dawned on me that I had been gone for all of three years, and if that were so I must now be fifteen summers old; though how such strangeness had come about I dared not ask. It was not just that my hair was longer or that I was taller, or that my old gown fitted me ill. My body too had changed. It was as if I had moved into a new house whose chambers I still felt too frightened to explore. Yet I found great comfort in the thought, for I had worked out that I had only been gone a short time in my mother's world, and maybe I had more time than I thought to take back the shadow.

Master Thankless said that it was beyond any rational explanation, though he was wise enough to keep this from his customers. Instead, he stitched together a story of my disappearance that held up well to the endless questioning from everyone who came into his shop. This is what he told them: I had run away from my house to try to find Mistress Danes.

When that proved impossible, I had gone to Hertfordshire where I had been taken in by a good Puritan family. I worked for them for three years before returning to London to see what had become of my father. In the hope of finding him I had stolen back into the house, but on hearing Arise Fell's voice I had hidden in the chest, and that was where I was found.

'I have heard that she was locked in there for six months,' one would say.

'No, longer,' another would reply. 'I have been told it was at least a year.'

Master Thankless would silence them all by saying firmly, 'I can assure you it was but a matter of hours, if that.'

He would give no more away, no matter how hard they pressed him. I thought Danes would be proud of her friend the tailor.

It soon became clear that Gabriel could hardly bear to be away from Hester, and Hester, for her part, fretted if he was not around. This meant that Gabriel had little time for his work.

'I am sorry, master,' said Gabriel, looking crestfallen. 'The trouble is that I am much fond of Hester.'

Master Thankless laughed. 'I would never have thought so, lad.'

Gabriel lowered his voice. 'Also, I worry in case those two villains come back for her.'

'Why would they?' I asked.

'Because Hester is the only witness to what they have been up to,' said Master Thankless.

'No, she is not,' I said. 'There is Joan, the cook. She must have seen it all.'

Master Thankless put his hand on my arm. 'Coriander, Joan is dead.'

'How? Of what?' I asked.

'She fell down the stairs,' said Master Thankless.

'Pushed, more likely,' said Gabriel. 'That's what I mean. I think they would kill Hester if they thought they could get away with it.'

It was hard to take in what he was saying. I was still shocked at hearing of Joan's death.

After that Gabriel was allowed to keep Hester company while I took his place in the shop. Soon Hester began to eat again and the colour came back to her cheeks.

Gabriel took great delight in bringing Hester all sorts of gifts and little oddments he had found. Hester kept them by her bed and treasured even the smallest. I think she had never been given a present in her life before.

'Was it Hester who told you what had happened to me?' I asked Master Thankless one evening as we worked late getting a gown ready for one of his customers.

'Yes, in the end, but to begin with it was Mistress Danes,' said the tailor. 'She came straight to me after Arise had thrown her out of the house. She was in a terrible state and I could make neither head nor tail of what she was telling me, other than that she was worried sick for you and intended to find Master Hobie to tell him what was going on. I did my best to persuade her to stay, and told her she could live here, but she said that was impossible: there was not a moment to be lost. To my eternal sorrow, I never saw her again.'

This was as much as Master Thankless would say. He seemed reluctant to talk of what had happened in my absence, as if he too found it hard to believe that I truly had been gone for so long. I made matters no better, for I would tell him nothing of my adventure, feeling that it was wise to hold my peace. So it was that we bobbed and curtsied around one another, until at last I was able to make sense of the missing years, and pieced together from bits of information given to me by Gabriel and the tailor a patchwork of the past.

After Danes had left, Master Thankless had become so concerned by all that he had heard that he had taken matters into his own hands and gone to Thames Street to enquire after me, only to be sent away again with a flea in his ear and one of Arise's sermons ringing in his head. Poor man, he was desperate for news of me, but what could he do? He had no proof that anything was amiss, other than customers' tittle-tattle, and that didn't make a bobbin's worth of thread.

Then Joan fell and died. It was then that all sorts of dreadful rumours began to go around and he became most fretful, for only Hester had ever been seen going to market, and neither hide nor hair had been seen of me. He was on the verge of reporting Maud to the authorities when the good ladies from

Arise's meeting house in Ludgate put it about that I was alive and well and had been brought to the ways of the Lord by Arise Fell himself, for I had had a fair devil in me that needed taming. A little while later Arise with great piety let it be known that, alas, all his hard work had been for naught, for I had run away in search of Danes. According to Master Fell, she was an evil woman, a witch, and I as her apprentice no better.

That would have been the sum total of Master Thankless's knowledge if it had not been for Gabriel. As Master Thankless said, 'Young Appleby is many things, but a tailor he will never be. A spy, now, that is a very different matter. There you have a brave one and no mistake. He set to the task of watching the house in Thames Street with more enthusiasm than he has ever shown for stitches.'

This was in August. It was hot, according to the tailor, and the Thames smelt none too sweet when two bodies were dragged from the river near Twickenham, the reeds having held them under for months. There was much talk as to who these two dead people could be, until Maud claimed it was me and Danes. It was a bleak day, said Master Thankless, who in his heart believed none of their nonsense, and gave Gabriel his blessing to find out what he could.

Gabriel, in borrowed cloak and tall hat, had gone to the meeting house in Ludgate, where he had been most surprised to find so much handsome furniture that seemed oddly out of place. He felt certain that this must be my father's property, though why it should be here and not sold for good coin he did not know.

There was little more to report until the day Arise and Maud had a visitor. He came, so Gabriel found out, by coach from Bristol. He was the one and only visitor they had had to the house, and such was the occasion that they sent Hester out to market alone. That was when Gabriel first got to speak to her, though she fair shook with fright and twisted and turned as if the very walls had eyes and ears to see and hear her by. She told him that the visitor was a lawyer called Tarbett Purman. She spoke of her deepest fears, of strange noises she had heard in the house, creakings and groanings. She was certain that the bodies found in the river were not mine or Danes's, sure that my grave lay closer to home, in my father's study.

Gabriel, feeling certain that Hester was in danger, climbed over the garden wall, hoping to see her a second time. They met and talked. After that, Hester disappeared. Gabriel became desperate, saying that he was sure that both of us were in the chest. The tailor once again had no evidence to act upon, until a letter from Master Bedwell arrived at the shop, dated long after the bodies had been pulled from the river. That was how he knew for certain that Danes had not been drowned, for the Bedwells had seen her and wondered if all was well, they being abroad in France and unable to do more than make enquiries.

On hearing all this, how I wished that I was a boy like Gabriel, for then I would have a chance of finding the shadow on my own and saving Tycho. Instead I felt useless, and all I could say was 'What would we have done without you, Master Thankless?'

'In truth, it is Gabriel you should thank more than me,' said Master Thankless. 'Now, will you allow me to ask you a question?'

'Of course.'

'How is it that you survived three years in a chest with neither food nor water?'

'Danes once told me the world is a mystery wrapped in a prayer,' I said. 'Please do not ask me where I have been, for I cannot say.'

'That tells me nothing. I see you are going to hold your peace on this. I will say one thing, though. I knew that day when you were little and went missing near my shop that there was something special about you. Those silver shoes of yours and the remedies your mother made. Such magic as that does not belong to this world of the Cross and crucifixion.'

*I*t was not long before Maud Leggs came waddling into the shop. She had become so large that she had to enter sideways. With the voice of a fishwoman rather than that of the wife of a respectable merchant, she began to shout abuse at Master Thankless.

'Mistress, please,' said Master Thankless, 'remember who you are.'

For a moment that settled her, at least long enough for Gabriel and me to clear the shop of its startled customers and close the door.

'I want to see my daughter,' said Maud. Her voice was so loud that it could be heard all through the house and halfway along the bridge.

'Please keep your voice down, mistress. Your daughter is still poorly.'

'I care naught for that. She be faking it so that she can get out of working. I want her home with me.'

'No one will be coming home with you today, mistress, nor tomorrow nor the next day,' said Master Thankless.

'I demand to see my daughter,' said Maud again.

'If you please, mistress, this is my shop and I do not want you in it. Now leave.'

'Hester, you miserable girl, you come down this minute or I will give you such a beating,' bellowed Maud, taking no notice of Master Thankless.

'If you do not go,' said Master Thankless, 'I will call the constable. I am sure he will be pleased to have a word with you.'

'Go on then,' said Maud. 'Call him. I am not afraid of a miserable little stitch-and-pin like you.'

'I should hope not,' said Master Thankless. 'And neither should you be afraid to tell the constable where all Master Hobie's furniture and fine wines have gone.'

Maud went very quiet.

'Gabriel,' said Master Thankless, 'will you be so kind as to fetch the constable?'

'Wait,' said Maud. 'Less haste. There be no need for that.

155

As you know, the Lord is most particular about his furniture, being offended by turned legs and any form of decoration. Arise Fell says it be as close to Sodom and Gomorrah as you are likely to come, and he should know.'

'I suppose he should,' said Master Thankless. 'And he found the wines no less displeasing?'

'Oh no,' said Maud, 'we drank those. I mean —'

'And the Good Lord has no objection to your beating and half-starving your daughter and locking your stepdaughter in a chest?'

'You devil!' snapped Maud. 'You twist my words, that you do.'

'No, mistress,' said Master Thankless, 'it is you who are twisted, not my words. Now I would like you to leave.'

She huffed, she puffed, she stamped her fat feet on the floor. 'I will be back, damn you, so I will. You have no rights over me and my own,' she shouted as she slammed the shop door shut. The bell went on jangling long after she had gone.

Master Thankless and I went upstairs to find Hester sitting up in bed, looking pale and shaken.

'I would rather die than go back there,' she said.

'I will not hear of it. This house is yours,' said Master Thankless. 'Over my dead body will you ever be treated like that again.'

'I will kill both of them if they so much as touch you,' declared Gabriel, and he said it with so much passion that we all burst out laughing. Even Hester managed a smile, while

Gabriel looked rather red in the face.

Later that day, as I sat beside her, Hester said, 'I have been thinking that written words are mighty powerful, more so than talking and telling.'

'Yes, I believe you are right,' I said.

'Arise can win any quarrel with words he takes from the Good Book. For they are smart, those words. They can be used to mean one thing one way, but then a person can use the same words to mean something quite different.'

'Words can be twisted to mean anything,' I said.

'That must be harder to do if they are written.'

'Yes,' I agreed. 'It is harder if they are written.'

'Would you mind writing down my words so they can be my shield against all the lies that have been told and all the wrong that has been done? Would you do that for me?'

'And more,' I said.

Hester nodded and lay back on the pillows.

These are Hester's words; this is Hester's story.

20

Hester

I was raised by my mother's hand and my father's pity. He was a tall man without a grain of ill humour, unlike my mother who was filled to the brim with anger.

We had a smallholding on the edge of the Forest of Savernake, with chickens and four sheep and a cow for milk. My mother gave birth more times than the cow, though the calves outlived near all my brothers and sisters, who went back into the earth like unfolded flowers. Only one brother, Ned, survived, he being six summers older than I. Ned used to stand up to my mother so that she was much thwarted in her rages.

This was how we lived, muddling along, ruled by my mother's temper. I think my father was glad when the war came and he could escape.

I did not want him to go. I begged him not to leave. My father hugged me and said it was his duty to go and fight so that all men could be free. In the eyes of the Lord all men were equal, he said, and so it should be on earth.

My mother did not stop him, saying she was well rid of his

slow ways. My father went off to join Cromwell's army, and you could not blame him for it. He said a thousand Royalists would be hard pushed to match my mother when the temper was upon her.

We were left, Ned and me, to keep our smallholding going. My mother being too large to touch her toes took instead to sitting by the fire raging. If the pot was empty she threatened to kill my father when he returned for leaving her with so little provision. Ned and I worked as hard as we could so that he might live. It was no use. I need not have worried about what my mother would do to him, for my father went missing at the Battle of Naseby and was thought to be dead.

My mother, so accustomed to loss, took no heed of this other than to say that she now be free, and she had an itch to see the city, where there was good coin to be made. My heart, like Ned's, not being as strong as my mother's, fair broke with grief.

Our neighbours, the Worts, had a son who like my father had been reported dead. In spite of that, he had come home fit and well, though a bit bruised around the head, some months later. Ned would not hear of our leaving, no matter how much my mother battered him with her ill temper. He stood fast, and we worked the land together, and looked after the animals as best we could. It was a cold wind that blew, those lean years after my father had gone.

Then into our lives crept the crooked man. He called himself a preacher and a prophet, and gave sermons that made people fair quake with fright. My mother took to bringing him home and feeding him with what little we had. Ned told her he had not worked this hard to give it all away.

At last we heard that my father was alive. He was most poorly, having lost a leg in the fighting. Ned and I felt our prayers had been answered, and Ned was all for setting off straight away to bring him home. I imagined then our troubles to be at an end, and that my father would see off the crooked man. It was not to be. My mother would not hear of Ned leaving.

'A man with one leg is good for naught,' she said. 'Anyway, he is sure to be dead by the time you find him, and then even more good coin will have been wasted.'

I tell you truly, it caused a terrible argument between them, and so angry and furious were my mother's words to Ned that I thought our cottage would come tumbling down. I hid with the animals, and when it was over Ned had gone. He had said he would come back with my father, but he did not and I knew not what to do.

My mother must have washed their names from her heart, for she never talked of them again. The words on her tongue were only for Arise. He told her that King Jesus would shortly reign over England and that we must all make ready for his return, and cleanse the land of its witches and cunning folk who do nothing but work for the Devil.

Arise had a way with words and my mother was mighty taken with him. She told me she would follow him wherever he did wander, and as he made his living by travelling she was all for going with him. I begged her not to leave, and she told me I could stay and starve if that was what I wanted.

We sold the sheep, the cow and the chickens, not getting good coinage for them as they were old and good for naught but meat, and they being skinny, when all was said and done, there was little of that either.

We set off towards Bristol and stayed in the countryside, my mother changing back to her maiden name of Leggs, Jarret being my father's name.

Arise Fell had as much wrath about him as she did, which greatly pleased her. She reckoned that if wrath be the Lord's fighting tool then she would willingly take up the sword and do battle.

It was Arise who told her that she had lost all her babies on account of evil charms brought about by a witch.

'But there be no witches where we live,' said my mother.

Arise stood up and banged the table so hard with his fist that I near jumped out of my skin.

'That is the way of cunning women and witches. They hide in villages. I will find them, wherever they are. I will leave no stone unturned,' he roared.

My mother did not move, but a smile spread across her face.

'Now do I remember the Worts and how their son came back home from the wars when all the other menfolk had been killed. My nose always told me there was something fishy about that woman.'

'What more proof do you need? There is your witch,' said Arise.

My mother looked like the cat that had got the cream. 'That were how my babies died and no mistake, all because of that woman's witchcraft.'

I thought my brothers' and sisters' deaths were more to do with her rages and the way she struck them when they cried, but I held my tongue.

Anyway, that was when the trouble began. Arise told my mother that had all she had to do was use that powerful nose of hers to smell out a witch.

My mother sniffed a lot: always had done, it being a habit that she could not help. And wiped her nose on her sleeve. Arise told her she was not to do that any more, and gave her a cloth. She should hold it to her nose and it did not matter her blowing into it as long as it be white.

'Witches are dirty,' said Arise. 'Godly folk are clean.'

He bought both of us new black skirts and jackets and black cloaks, so that we went about the countryside looking like crows.

From then on we followed Arise wherever the Good Lord saw fit to lead him. Folk took him and my mother for husband and wife. I was thought to be Arise's daughter and my mother did not say otherwise.

They caused terror and trembling wherever they went. In each village and hamlet Arise would put the fear of God into the congregation. So dreadful were his sermons that many women fainted, which my mother, with a sniff of her nose, took to be the first sign of the Devil at work. For there is one thing the Devil cannot abide, so said Arise, and that is the name of the Good Lord said out loud.

Word spread about the preacher and all feared him, and that he would take their money for Maud not to accuse their wives and daughters of being witches. There was good coinage to be made for Arise in finding witches, for many a father and husband, brother or uncle would pay dear for my mother not to sniff too hard.

I am ashamed of the trouble that we caused. I wanted no part in it and things with my mother and me went bad.

Summer passed and winter was upon us. It was a hard time and no mistake, what with the war and few farmers left to till the soil, and many men made their way to the cities in hope of employment.

On Christmas Day we came to a hamlet where Arise was to preach. Only one person saw fit not to come and listen, an old woman who was poorly. My mother's nose found her out and Arise denounced her as a witch. She begged Arise to leave her and be gone, but this was like meat and bread to Arise and my mother. They went into the house and dragged that poor frail woman from her sickbed. With much preaching and shouting that they must be vigilant to withstand the Devil, they took her down to the river, where Arise raised his hand of wrath and struck her hard.

I implored my mother to leave well alone, and she punched me in the face so that I fell to the ground. I got up again as Arise took to beating the woman round the head with the hand of wrath and a stick until she fell. My mother then in a passion of rage took to kicking her. It was a shameful sight. She was thrown in the icy water and sank like a stone. That showed she must be innocent, for if she had risen to the surface they would have known that she was a witch. I think that be right. Either way I know that you do not come out of the water alive.

After that the villagers went into their houses and barred their doors against us. They took no notice of Arise when he threatened them with damnation. No one asked us in and we were forced to leave.

It was a cold night with a powerful icy wind that found its way to your bones. My mother and Arise were both now quiet, having used their strength to kill a frail old woman.

I walked behind with tears rolling down my face, thinking of my kind sweet father and my loving brother Ned. I wished then that I had been a boy so that I could have fallen and died honourably in battle.

We went on in this manner until we came to Bristol. None of us having the energy to go further, we took rooms at a coach house near the main thoroughfare.

21

The Strange Lady

I was much pleased with our lodgings, for they were clean, but alas, they were not to my mother's or Arise's liking, for too many travellers stayed there, bringing with them tales of witch hunts. Then came the news of the murder of a sick, old, defenceless woman who had been kicked and beaten, then left to drown on Christmas Day. On hearing this Arise became as jumpy as a fox's tail full of fleas, sure that the hangman was following him. So we left those lodgings before any, one remembered it be a green-eyed twisted preacher who had dragged the old woman out of her house, and we went further into town and rented rooms above a tavern. It was a noisy, dirty place full of vermin, and it was a struggle to keep clean.

It was not long before the money Arise had got from witch hunting was gone, for my mother had a great hunger on her, and Arise a great thirst, and between them they spent what there was. Each blamed the other for their woes, and my mother fair shouted at him that he best think of a way of earning some money and be smart about it, for she had not come all this way to starve.

Arise went every evening not to the meeting house but to the tavern downstairs, coming back to our room with the liquor upon him, ranting and raving about the reign of Jesus Christ. 'He is on his way. Do you hear that, woman, on his way!'

Shortly after that, when our very last coin was gone, Arise brought Tarbett Purman back to our room.

Tarbett Purman reminded me of an eel, at any rate something slippery that lived a lot in dark places.

'This is Hester,' said Arise, all preacher-like, putting the hand of salvation and the hand of wrath together like a church steeple.

Master Purman told me to stand before him. Then he asked me to turn around slowly, which I did.

'I like them bigger on the rump, bigger in the stomach, bigger in the breast – in short, a buxom wench,' he said, grabbing my mother's waist. 'I like a proper woman.'

This pleased my mother, who took to laughing. It also pleased Arise, for Master Purman put a coin on the table.

Tarbett Purman became a regular visitor. When he was away on business, Arise would come home with some other godly gentleman who had sworn to the cause of ridding England of sinners, and he too would put a coin on the table.

Most evenings that cold winter I spent huddled out of sight on the steps of our lodgings.

My mother spent her days in bed, eating and sleeping, while

I tried to keep the room clean. It was the only time that the wrath quietened in her.

I begged often that we might go home.

'To what?' she said. 'A hovel where the earth be full of my dead children? I think not. Thanks to Arise, here we have food and good coin.'

I thought that this was the way my world was set to turn and there was naught I could do about it.

Then one day a lady asked to see my mother. I thought it might be Tarbett Purman's wife for I doubted not that he had one. She wore a cloak cut of the finest wool and stood out amongst the vagabonds, travellers and masterless men who had rooms there.

'Go and tell your mother to dress, girl,' she said, and I wondered how she knew that my mother would still be in bed, it being the middle of the day.

I rushed up the stairs and told my mother that I thought Tarbett Purman's wife be wanting to see her. She heaved herself out of bed saying she would give the woman a piece of her mind, so she would. It was hard getting my mother dressed, she complaining that I must have shrunk the bodice and the skirt, for they hardly met in the middle. I did my best to straighten out the bed, but the lady came up before I could finish.

There was something about this lady that made me fearful, though what it was I could not say.

I asked if I should take her cloak and dry it for her. She said no and sat down by the fire, so that steam rose off her clothes. My mother for once looked at a loss as to what to say, for this was without doubt a grand lady.

'You are to be married,' she said to my mother.

My mother was dumbstruck and had no words sitting on her tongue.

'Me?' she said when she found her voice. 'I think I still be married.'

'That is a mortal detail. It seems not to bother you, so why should it bother me?'

'But – but –' said my mother.

'Silence, Maud Jarret,' said the lady, 'and listen.'

'How do you know my name?' said my mother.

'I know your name and I know your nature. You and that preacher have been making much trouble,' said the lady, laughing.

'He be nothing to do with me,' said my mother, backing away from the lady. 'I be a good God-fearing –'

'You are a trollop,' said the visitor, 'a slut. I know all about you. I know what you and Arise Fell have done. I understand all too well how things lie between you.'

Here my mother took to babbling. The lady in the cloak never once raised her voice. She said, as if saying no more than it be Tuesday, 'You are a murderer.'

'No I am not! I am not!' pleaded my mother, falling to her knees. 'I was led astray.'

'Get up and stop your whimpering,' said the visitor curtly. 'Who you kill concerns me not. So long as you do as you are told no one else will ever know what you have done. Do you understand me, Maud Jarret?'

My mother nodded. 'Whatever you say.'

'You are to bathe and make yourself presentable.'

'Nay, mistress. I never bathe,' said my mother. 'Water brings on the distemper.'

'You will do as you are told, so that you smell less of stale fish.'

'That be the smell of witches,' said my mother, crossing her arms.

The lady in the chair laughed. 'Then that nose of yours has smelt nothing more or less than yourself.'

Instead of shouting and screaming my mother just stood there looking frightened.

'He is a rich merchant, a widower with one daughter,' the lady said.

My mother came nearer, the word 'rich' drawing her on.

'Why would he be bothered with me?' she asked.

'In other times nothing in this world would make him bother with you, but Oliver Cromwell has seen fit to take away the lands and possessions of those Royalists who supported the King, and this gentleman has a very desirable residence on the River Thames. To keep it, he must be seen to be a good Republican. To this end he needs an honest Puritan wife.' She laughed once more. 'You are exactly what I have been looking for: you will be no threat to the memory of his beloved. Just do your duty and keep quiet. That is all that is asked of you.'

'I have an itching desire to see London,' said my mother, 'but I cannot leave Arise.'

'Neither would I want you to,' said the lady. 'Arise will join you later.'

My mother still looked uncertain, but when the lady took a bag of gold coins from her cloak and threw them on the floor, she fell upon them like a pig at the trough.

'Clean yourself up,' said the lady, standing tall over my mother. 'Have clothes made to fit. Go to church. For the time being, see little of Arise and his friends. Leave the rest to me. Remember, you are a widow, an upstanding widow with an only daughter. Do you understand?'

Her cloak now seemed to have green vapours coming from it, though it may just have been the way the light from the door played upon it. My mother did not even look up. She was still grabbing at the gold coins as the lady left.

That night the lady came back again and told me I was to stay outside while she talked to Maud and Arise. I was pleased, having no desire to listen to the tricks and foolery Arise would come up with. I sat on the steps and watched a large black raven hop about, leaving its tracks in the snow.

The next morning a finely dressed servant came to take us to our new lodgings. Oh, you should have seen them! Never had I lived anywhere so grand until I came to London. There were two maids and a cook. New gowns were ordered and my mother with much shouting and screeching was bathed and her hair washed to rid her of lice and fleas. It was the same for me, which I liked a lot for now my skin itched no more and my bites at last began to heal.

My mother caught a chill and needed victuals brought to her in bed, and sweetmeats to keep the distemper away. Then we went once more to church and I did a lot of praying that we might never see Arise again. We fasted too, for the lady with the cloak wanted there to be less of my mother when she met your father.

My mother did not take well to fasting and the servants had to lock her in her chamber, where she would shout until too weak to go on. The servants took no notice. They were not interested in her fire and brimstone. They said nothing.

So we lived, seeing no one, going about our ways quietly together, and taking to washing and being clean in both body and mind.

Then your father came to visit us. I think he was fair surprised to see the size of my mother and the thinness of her hair. She told him it was all due to the losing of her dear husband. He said that he understood the power of grief, his love being only three months dead. His eyes filled up with tears when he said this.

I am not good at counting, but I believe that we lived in that house for six months. If that be true, it means that the lady in the cloak could see into the future, for your mother must still have been alive on the day of her visit to our lodgings.

I only saw your father that once before the wedding. He seemed pleased to see it was a clean house and that my mother did not smell, even though her teeth were black. That is how we came to London.

I was sure that you would not like me for coming into your house so soon after your mother's death. I told myself not to worry if that be so. Then when you were so kind and sweet I could not believe that the Good Lord had seen fit to give me such a sister as you. I knew that I would love you always.

If I could have wished for one thing that day we first met, it would have been that my mother had never entered your house. I knew the damage her wrath would cause and I prayed every night for the Lord to keep us safe and not let Arise Fell come here. The Good Lord did not answer my prayers.

*Y*ou know what followed, until that dreadful day when your hair was scissored from your head. Well, after Arise had dragged you upstairs into the study and all the banging had died down, Joan and I set to cleaning the kitchen and putting the meat upon the spit, both quietly praying that Arise would see fit to let you down to the kitchen that evening. It was not to be. Nor the next day, and I knew not what to make of it. I asked both Arise and my mother to let you go before any more harm befell you, but I was beaten soundly for my trouble and told to mind my own business.

I took to making a mark under the beam in the attic for every day you were gone. I did the marks in rows of seven and crossed the mark every time it was a Sunday. All I know is that there were too many Sundays, which made me think you must be dead.

Joan was never the same after you were gone. She took to crying and bemoaning her fate, saying that she was not paid nor fed nor housed as she should be. Arise took her few things and threw them into the river. He told her she was so vexatious that there was no salvation for her.

Shortly after this, poor Joan missed her footing on the cellar steps and was badly hurt. Arise would not go to the expense of calling Doctor Turnbull. Instead, he told her to pray that the Good Lord would see fit to mend her. I helped her up to bed and she lay there groaning in pain. My mother came puffing and panting up the attic stairs and shouted at her to stop her noise.

Joan saw her only chance of escape and took it. She died the next morning. Arise and my mother seemed fair pleased to see her body taken away on a cart. I watched her go, sure that I would be next.

After that there was only me to keep the big house going and I did my best, but there were too many chambers and too many fires and too many stairs so that I lost all sense of time. There was to be no rest or peace in the house and I felt fair terrified at what was to befall me.

Then my mother and Arise told me, as if it were the same as a Sunday, that you and Mistress Danes had been found in the river, and that was the end of the matter. In my heart I did not believe them, but I bit my tongue and kept my silence.

Our lives went on. The furniture was taken away bit by bit, and the house was silent and cold. Arise took to locking rooms up and going off to the alehouse leaving my mother to grumble about her fate, saying that it was not fair after all she had done to be left so. Late at night, we would hear creakings and groanings coming from the house. My mother, never one bothered with imagination, would look frightened and ask who I thought it might be. I had no answer but my fear became all the greater.

My mother was made merrier when Tarbett Purman came up to London. For the first time I was sent to market on my own to buy what was needed to feed our guest. Arise struck me before I left, saying that the hand of wrath would be waiting for me if I should dawdle.

That was the first time I met Master Gabriel Appleby. I was mighty scared in case anyone saw us talking. Then, much to my surprise, he climbed over the garden wall to see me again. I was near lost for words, but I took what courage I had and told him everything, and the worst of it was that I was sure you were dead. He was so kind, and I just wanted to rest my head on his shoulder. He said he would take me back to Master Thankless's with him, but I knew my legs would never make it.

Then Master Thankless and the sea captain came to the door.

22

Green Fire

'*T*hat is all I have to say,' said Hester. 'I hope my words stand tall and straight and speak the honest truth for me.'

'Hester, they do more than that,' I said. 'They show you are brave and true like your father.'

Hester's eyes filled with tears. 'I regret much that I did not speak to your father and tell him the truth,' she sobbed.

'He would not have heard you in a thousand years of headless kings,' I said, 'for all he could hear was the sound of his own grief.'

Hester's words stood more than tall and straight. They were like spears that went through me.

My mother was still alive when Rosmore told Maud to marry my father. What part had she played in my mother's death? My heart sank, for I knew then, as clear as light, that she was after the shadow. I did not know where it was, for the last time I had seen it it had been in the ebony casket, and I knew the study was now empty.

I willed Hester to get better with all speed, so that I could get back to Thames Street.

Winter had passed and spring made its welcome return. The river thawed and flooded the banks on the Southwark side, giving the ferrymen employment after the frozen winter.

It was not only the river that had thawed. The customers who came to the shop were beginning to talk more openly while choosing their fabrics and having their gowns fitted. They even dared to grumble about the closure of the theatres and the banning of Christmas and the maypole. Last spring such talk would have been thought dangerous. I began to hope that maybe now it was safe for my father to come home.

Master Thankless, swept up with the moment, took the Bible from the counter and put it away in a drawer and talked about hanging up his old sign, the one that said *By Appointment to the King*. Other more solemn gentlemen who came to have their black doublets fitted argued that Cromwell was a stronger man and people were very much mistaken if they thought he would not take the crown for himself.

'Why would we want another king when we have one alive and well and living as poor as a church mouse in Holland?' said others.

I loved listening to all the talk. As Master Thankless said, there was nothing so good for bringing out the tittle-tattle as the fitting of gowns and doublets. The best gossip was about Arise and Maud, and I enjoyed much hearing how the mighty had fallen.

'Who would believe that she would let the house get into that state?'

'I heard all the furniture was gone.'

'What was she thinking of, I should like to know, letting that crooked preacher live with her?'

'And when you think of Mistress Eleanor Hobie, such a kind and lovely lady! She helped me with my ague.'

'And the daughter is sick in bed. No one knows if she'll walk again.'

Then they would whisper very quietly, 'And what about Coriander? Can you explain that one to me, my dear?'

And all would end up saying, 'What would Master Hobie say if he were here?'

Then one bitterly cold night I was woken by Gabriel, who said that he had seen green flames coming from my house. I got dressed with all haste and went down to the shop. From the back window you could clearly see Thames Street, though nothing looked amiss.

'Forgive me,' said Gabriel. 'I should not have alarmed you, though on my life I swear I saw green flames.'

'I believe you,' I said, and taking our cloaks we went out into the street. All was deserted. A thin veil of powdery snow lay undisturbed over the cobbles.

'Who goes there?' we heard someone call. 'Is that you, Appleby?'

'Yes,' shouted Gabriel as the night watchman came into view.

'Thought as much,' he said, holding up his lantern. 'And who is your companion?'

'Coriander Hobie.'

'And what brings you two out on such a night?'

'I have seen flames coming from Thames Street,' said Gabriel.

'I have just come back from there myself. I saw them too,' said the night watchman. 'All most strange. But there is no fire, as far as I can tell.'

Snow had started to fall and I began to shiver and my teeth to chatter.

'Come on with you both,' said the night watchman kindly. 'It is too cold to be standing out here talking.'

He took us back to his gatehouse and sat us down in front of a warm fire. 'I tell you I will be a happy man to see daylight,' he said, as he handed us two mugs of hot toddy and took once more to looking up and down Bridge Street. 'I should not say this,' he went on, 'but I am mighty pleased to have your company, for this night has fair given me the frights, even set the hairs on the back of my dog to stand upright. Never seen him so affected.'

The dog lay by the fire looking towards the door, while his master told us what he had seen.

The night watchman had just called twelve o'clock when he heard the sound of a carriage coming over the bridge from the Southwark side. He went to have a look, for it was going at quite a lick and the street was slippery on account of the snow.

'I have not seen so grand a carriage for a long time,' said the night watchman. 'It was pulled by four mighty handsome midnight black horses, and the coachmen wore red.'

'Where did it go?' I asked, feeling a chill run down my spine.

'That's what makes me think it must be the Devil,' said the night watchman. 'It vanished, didn't it, as it got towards the City end of the bridge. God be my witness, for I do not tell a lie, it did not leave one mark in the snow, nothing to show it had ever passed. Now my missus, she's one for believing in the fairies and all sorts, but not me. I have no time for that nonsense, though I tell you truly I can make not head nor tail of what I saw.'

With a beating heart I asked, 'Did the carriage come back again?'

'No,' said the night watchman.

'Did you see anything else?' asked Gabriel.

'A raven. That is what I saw, didn't I?' he said. 'A monstrous great black raven flew after the carriage. It made my flesh creep. What do you make of that?'

What I made of it I could not tell him, for I felt too alarmed by all he had said.

'Strange indeed,' said Gabriel.

We were just saying our farewells when a constable appeared at the door. He too seemed most agitated.

'Did you see green flames coming from Thames Street?' he asked.

'I did,' said the night watchman, 'and so did young Appleby.'

'All most odd,' said the constable. 'I just came back from there, though I could see no sign of any fire. The neighbours said they had seen green flames, and a black carriage standing outside the house.'

'Did you see the carriage?' asked Gabriel.

'No,' said the constable, 'and I do not think there ever was a carriage, for there were no wheel marks in the snow.'

We left the night watchman and the constable talking, and made our way back to the tailor's shop. As we turned the door handle, I fair jumped out of my skin to hear the squawk of a bird. I turned round to see the raven fly away out over the river. Never had I felt more fear than I did then, for I knew, and had known the minute the night watchman had told us about the carriage, that its passenger was none other than Queen Rosmore, in search of the shadow.

'Are you all right?' asked Gabriel. 'You look pale. Were you frightened?'

'No,' I said. 'It is just tiredness.' And went back to my bed, though I did not sleep again. Instead I lay awake wondering what to do and knowing that time was running out. I had to get back to my house on Thames Street, but how?

I remembered my father saying that the river is never the same, that it is always changing, each tide bringing in the new, sucking out the old, though on the surface nothing seems altered. So it was with me. Just when I felt at my lowest ebb, when I knew not what to do, everything changed once more. For into Master Thankless's shop came Danes.

*A*nd so the fourth part of my tale is told, and with it another candle goes out.

PART FIVE

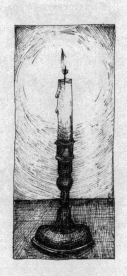

23
Confessions

On the evening of Danes's return, Master Thankless sent Nell out to buy one of Mistress Garnet's venison pies.

'Only the best, mind you,' he said.

'There is no need to go to all this trouble,' said Danes.

'Nonsense,' said Master Thankless cheerfully, putting up the shutters and closing the door on the day's business. 'Today is a day for celebration, for you have come home to us.'

I could not let Danes out of my sight, worried that if I did she might disappear again. Master Thankless, seeing how anxious I was to talk to her alone, said, 'Coriander, make yourself useful and show Mistress Danes to her chamber.'

I took her upstairs and we sat by the window overlooking the river.

'What a beauty you are,' she said. 'You look so like your mother. Oh, my sparrow, it has been the longest and thinnest of times. I near lost heart that I would ever see you again.'

'Where have you been?' I asked.

Danes shook her head. 'I went to France, then to the

Netherlands, in search of your father. Alas, I never found him, but not for the lack of trying. Finally, I stumbled on Master and Mistress Bedwell. They offered to help, though when all is said and done there was little they could do, for they too were afraid to go back to London. By then I felt I had wasted too much time and all that concerned me was getting back here again. Travel, as you know, is not easy. Now, I have said enough. Just let us leave it be.' She sighed and took my face in her hands. 'More to the point, my little sparrow, where did you fly off to?'

Checking that we were alone, I whispered what I knew and for the first time in this world said the names that I had been keeping locked away in my heart. I told her about Medlar, about Tycho, Queen Rosmore, and Cronus. I told her about King Nablus and Unwin, the summer palace and the wedding. I told her of the liquid mirror and the shadow.

She shuddered. 'I hate to think what would have happened to you if there had been no Medlar.'

'Do you know anything about my mother's past?' I asked.

Danes turned away and looked out of the window. Then she said very quietly, as if the words came not from her but from the breeze, 'I once saw her shadow.'

I felt the weather in me change, the heavy clouds lifting and breath filling my body once again.

When Danes told me what had happened three months before my mother died, it was as if a candle had been brought into a dark room, and I knew then, with a shock, that that must have been the time Rosmore first visited Maud.

She said that my mother was sitting staring at the ebony casket, certain that whatever was inside it had been stolen.

'I was fair worried,' said Danes. 'At last she unlocked the casket, and I saw a great light shining from it. I was mighty fascinated, until your mother lifted out something that looked like a piece of gossamer that shone from her hands and then sank into her skin. She began to fade away. I screamed her name. Then I saw her pull the gossamer away from her and push it back into the casket.'

'It was her fairy shadow,' I said.

'Your mother said the shadow had the power to take her back to the world she came from, and with all her heart she did not want to go. She told me that I had saved her by screaming. As if waking from a trance, she said she had seen the future. It seems that she had given the casket to your father on their wedding night, telling him to keep it safe and never give it back, or he would lose her. She made me promise to hold my peace, which I have done until now.'

'I have to find her shadow and take it back to Medlar,' I said. 'Without it Tycho will be killed. The shadow has more power in it than can be left in the hands of charlatans like Arise and Maud.'

'The one thing I know, my sparrow, is that your mother loved you and your father and never wanted to leave you. I have thought a lot about this, for it has been a mighty puzzle with so many pieces missing, and I think those silver shoes must have come from the other world. She was all for throwing them into the river, for she did not want you to have them, but like you I could see no harm in them.'

'My mother was right,' I said. 'I have often thought that if I had let well alone, she might still be alive.' And I felt tears well up and a lump in my throat.

Danes wrapped me in her arms and we sat there, both of us quiet, both of us thinking and listening to noises from the street: hawkers, the cries of the ferryman, the water wheels churning, and I felt the tide once more changing.

Downstairs in the parlour the table had been laid with a white cloth, a fire was ablaze in the grate and candles burnt brightly. We all sat down to a feast like kings and queens of old. When we had finished eating, Master Thankless took out his lute and we sang and danced and were as merry as if it were Christmas Day.

24

The Storm

Summer came on and the weather got steadily hotter until London seemed to be covered in a thick blanket of unbearable heat. All the windows of the shop and the living quarters front and back were open to let in what little breeze there was.

There had once again been an outbreak of the plague, as always when the weather is hot, and there was a panic that it could be as bad as last time. Danes told me it was truly dreadful, both her parents having died from it and she only being spared because she was working out in the wilds of the country.

Master Thankless took to going once a week to check the plague numbers that were printed out and put up in each parish. Every week the numbers rose and fear began to grip London. It had been foretold in no lesser book than the Bible that a great plague was coming, though I sensed that this was not it. Nevertheless, the rich and those with friends and relatives in the country took no chances. They locked their

London houses and had carriages, carts and barges take them far away from the city.

'Can one call this progress?' said Master Thankless as we watched the endless procession trundle past his shop and across London Bridge. 'Do you know that in good Queen Bess's day carriages were almost unheard of?' And he sighed as two coachmen screamed abuse at each other, both claiming they had right of way.

Every week the plague figures continued to rise. I had two hopes, one kinder than the other. The unkind hope, which almost became a prayer, was that Maud and Arise might be struck down with the deadly disease. The kinder one was that they would at least plan to leave London so that I could go back to the house.

It was not to be. Maud Leggs and Arise Fell stayed put like two ferrets in a hole.

Master Thankless said that the bridge was not a bad place to be because it had the luxury of a breeze. It was agreed that it would be best if we stayed together at least until the plague figures began to fall.

It was in the quiet days that followed that Hester told Danes the truth about Maud and Arise. When she had finished she looked mighty sad.

'Do you think I will turn out like my mother?' she asked.

Danes went over to her and took her gently in her arms as if she were a child. 'There, there,' she said. 'Do not fret. You are the sweetest flower that ever grew on a dunghill.'

All this time I had been weighed down by skirts and all that was expected of young ladies. Months had passed and I had done nothing to get the shadow back. More to the point, I had no way of knowing what to do.

I told Danes that I could not stay still any more. I had to think of something. 'I have let everyone down,' I said.

'Stop being such a ninny. You are not going to get anywhere if you think like that,' said Danes, rolling up her sleeves. It was Wednesday, her day for baking, and she started kneading the dough as if it was an argument that would not listen to reason.

It was hot in the kitchen, with the kind of heat that makes you want to sleep. My eyelids felt heavy and a thought came to me. What if Arise knew that the silvery gossamer thing in the casket had power over Rosmore, and that with it he could bargain for anything he wanted? If that were so, he would use it to wheedle as much out of her as he could.

Danes dusted her hands so that a cloud of flour drifted slowly and lazily in the sunlight. She went over to a stoneware jug, poured two cool tankards of elderflower ale and set them on the table. 'You are a sleepyhead,' she said to me, smiling. 'Come and sit yourself down.'

'It is too hot,' said Gabriel, coming into the kitchen. 'My head is crackling.'

'There is a storm in the air,' said Danes, getting up to pour him a drink.

'I wish I could borrow your clothes, Gabriel,' I said without thinking. 'If I were disguised as a boy I could go with you to spy on Thames Street. I could even get into the house from the river through the water gate.'

Gabriel laughed. 'You, dressed as a boy, with all those curls!'

Danes looked at me. 'It is not such a foolish notion.'

'You are jesting,' said Gabriel.

'No, I am not,' I said. My heart was now racing. Why, this was the salvation I had been looking for. Why had I not thought of it before?

'No,' said Gabriel. 'It is too dangerous.'

'Then I will go by myself.'

'I will not let you,' said Gabriel. 'They will have you back in that chest with a knife through your heart for good measure.'

'Now,' said Danes, 'we are all running away with ourselves.'

'Why do you want to get back into the house?' said Gabriel, taking no notice of her. 'Surely you should be glad to be well away from it.'

'I am. I am very pleased to be here. I would have been lost without Master Thankless. All the same there is something I need, something that belonged to my mother that must be returned to its rightful place.'

'Let sleeping dogs lie,' said Gabriel. 'There is nothing left in that house. Most of the furniture has been taken.'

'It is only a small casket,' I said.

Gabriel stood up. 'I am truly sorry for all that has befallen your family, but no good will come of your going back there,' he said sharply. 'Let it be.'

I remembered those words. My mother had said them to me

long ago over my silver shoes. But it was not the end then and neither would it be now.

I was thinking how best to win my case when the room suddenly went dark, as if the middle of the night was upon us. It was so gloomy that Danes lit the candles and pulled the windows to. Then there was a terrible rumble of thunder. The house shook and Nell came running down the stairs with her hands over her head to hide in fear under the table.

'It is the wrath of God coming to get us,' she whimpered.

I looked out of the window. Nature, I thought, could be more furious than any man's quarrel when she wished. As I watched, the sky, dark as boiling brimstone, was lit up by a flash of lightning that streaked yellow across the river.

'Where is Hester?' asked Gabriel, suddenly anxious.

'She has gone to take some baby gowns to Mistress Kent,' said Danes. 'She should be back soon. I told her I was baking her favourite seed cake.'

There was another crack of thunder and the rain began to fall.

'I will go and fetch her,' said Gabriel. 'She should not be out in weather like this.'

'Wait, for goodness' sake,' said Danes, 'at least until the worst of the storm is over.'

'Rain does not bother me,' said Gabriel.

'This ain't rain,' mumbled Nell, 'this is the flood coming. We're all going to be swept away.'

'They are as good as married,' said Danes as Gabriel left the room, and she took the seed cake from the oven, all golden and warm.

I went upstairs to help Master Thankless with the shutters. The tailor was standing in the doorway. The thunder rolled loud and low and the rain fell in draughtsman's lines, hitting the cobbles before dancing up again. We watched it wash away the filth in the gutter. A carriage passed by, the driver soaked to the skin. People were running for cover and huddling in door-ways, washing hung sodden between the two rows of houses and not one word could be heard, so loud was the noise of the rain. The storm had come without warning and the shopkeep-ers' goods were stranded on the roadway. Pamphlets from the printer's shop opposite had blown away and were floating in the puddles, the ink running and the words blurred.

'We shall all be drowned,' Nell had wailed. And I thought she might be right, for the water in the street and the water in the river looked as if they were one. Master Thankless shut the door to the shop and, taking my arm, led me downstairs.

'Is Gabriel not back yet?' asked Danes as we came into the kitchen.

'No, most probably he will stay with Hester at Mistress Kent's until the worst of this is over,' said Master Thankless, sitting down. 'Not good for business, this weather, but it will clear the air. Come, Nell,' he said kindly, 'there will be no seed cake for you while you remain hidden down there.'

Nell crept out and sat nervously at the table while the heav-ens continued to argue their case.

'Storms as sudden as this often foretell great events,' said Master Thankless.

'My mother told me they are brought over by witches who sail in sieves,' said Nell.

'Fiddle-faddle!' said Danes.

Just then the shop bell rang and Gabriel rushed down the stairs two at a time.

'She's gone,' he shouted. 'She has gone.'

'Slow down, lad,' said Master Thankless. 'Who's gone?'

'She never went to Mistress Kent.'

'What are you talking about?' asked the tailor.

'Hester,' wept Gabriel. 'Hester is gone.'

25

A New Suit of Clothes

I knew immediately what had happened. Hester had been kidnapped and taken back to Thames Street.

'But why?' said Master Thankless. 'What would they want with Hester now?'

'To make sure that she is silent,' said Danes grimly.

'This has been my worst fear all along,' said Gabriel. 'I will kill them for this!'

'Calm yourself, Gabriel,' said Danes firmly, putting both her hands on his shoulders. She took a little bottle from her apron pocket. 'Take this.'

He did so and sat down with his head in his hands. 'I love her,' he said. 'I cannot be without her.'

'I know,' said Danes, 'and we will get her back, but first we have to make a plan. No battle is ever won without one.'

Gabriel looked up. 'I have no plan,' he said miserably.

'I have,' I said. 'And for it, I will need a suit of boy's clothes that will fit me and a good cap that will hide my curls.'

Nell burst out laughing but then, seeing the solemn look on everyone's face, was quiet.

'Then what?' asked Master Thankless.

'I will go by boat to the water gate of my old house and see if I can get into it that way. I am certain I know which chamber Hester will be in.'

Master Thankless started to pace up and down and for one awful moment I was sure he was going to say no.

'Gabriel must go with you, then. I will not hear of you going by yourself. It is far too dangerous.'

'Coriander, if you are right and they already have Hester, what do you think they would do if they caught you as well?' said Gabriel. 'No, you show me how the house is laid out and where she will be and I will do this on my own.'

'You need me to be there,' I said, desperate for my voice to sound strong, for this was the chance I had been waiting for. I could not let it slip by. I had to get back and find the shadow. I had to.

'Gabriel, be quiet and listen to Coriander's plan,' said Master Thankless firmly. Suddenly I felt hopeful.

'Can you get a boat?' I asked.

Master Thankless nodded. 'I have a friend, a Master Starling. He will help us. Now, you are sure about this, Coriander?'

I wanted to shout 'Yes, yes, yes' but I managed to say it quietly.

'Then we had better get started,' said the tailor.

While my clothes were being made ready, I drew with great

care the plan of my house so that Gabriel could study it. We went through it time and time again.

'These are the stairs that lead to the attic,' I explained.

'Yes, and that door to the left was your old chamber,' said Gabriel, following the map with his finger.

'And the fifth step on the second landing creaks,' I added.

'As does the sixth step,' he said.

'Right!'

'I feel I know the house like the back of my hand now,' Gabriel said confidently. In truth, I felt less certain for it had been a long time since I had been there, but I kept this to myself.

Danes dressed me with care. A cap hid my hair and my pale skin was made darker with walnut oil. I dabbed more on to my chin and cheeks to show a shadow of where a beard might grow, so that when I looked in the glass I saw not myself but the image of a young lad.

Even Gabriel looked twice as I walked into the shop, doing my best to copy his stride.

'Coriander?' he said uncertainly.

'Yes, Gabriel,' I said.

'Well, blow me down, you look the part all right!'

And Nell, who had been upstairs all the while, came into the shop and became all flirtatious and skittish. She blushed scarlet when she realised who I was.

'Oh my! Who would have thought it?' she said. 'You make a mighty handsome lad, mistress, better even than Master Appleby.'

And for the first time that wretched day Gabriel, despite himself, smiled.

*I*t was dark and still raining when we set off. I felt nervous as we left, with Master Thankless and Danes anxiously watching us as we walked together down Bridge Street towards the church of St Magnus.

'Take this,' said Gabriel when we were at the top of Thames Street, and he handed me a dagger. I was so shocked by the glint of the blade that I all but dropped it.

'Just to be on the safe side,' Gabriel whispered.

I followed him, doing my best to keep my stride long. The freedom from skirts felt wonderful, though the weight of the dagger and all that it meant reminded me that this was no childish game.

We went past the tavern and down to the river steps and I suddenly wished that I was inside drinking ale and listening to watermen's tales rather than tackling the task in front of us.

'Are you ready?' asked Gabriel.

I nodded.

'You know you can still go back,' he said. 'It is not too late for a change of heart.'

I shook my head, scared to speak lest my voice betray me.

The waterman stood waiting for us on the bottom step.

'All well, Master Starling?' asked Gabriel.

He huffed. 'Now tell me, do people like to go on the river in weather like this? They do not! Not when for the same coin, head or tails of it, they can hire a carriage to take them on their journey in the dry.'

Gabriel handed Master Starling a purse. He tipped the coins into the palm of his huge hand.

'Very kind of you, sir. Much appreciated,' he said, handing Gabriel his lantern.

'We shall be back before the watch calls twelve,' said Gabriel, climbing into the boat.

'And who is this lad?' asked Master Starling, looking at me.

'A new apprentice,' said Gabriel, and I clambered on board, unused to doing so without a hand to hold.

'A bit green behind the ears,' said the waterman with a laugh, as he walked back up the steps towards the tavern. 'Do not give him the oars, or you will never get home!'

There is something overwhelming about the Thames that cannot be seen from the safety of land. It is a wild and raw river that has a will of its own, untamed by shorelines. I began to understand this as we were pulled downstream by the full force of its angry tide.

Gabriel rowed, doing his best to keep the boat close to the bank out of sight from the houses above us. The rain having now stopped, their windows were open, spilling out half-heard conversations that drifted down through the candlelight. A dog barked, its cry answered by another dog.

My house stood unlit. The water gate was deserted and dank, with green slime clinging to the steps.

'Perhaps they are not at home,' I said.

'They are there all right,' said Gabriel.

We moored the boat so that we were parallel to the gate. Gabriel stood up and tried to lift it. It would not move. He sat down again, dejected. 'Now what?' he said.

Suddenly, a green light shot out from the study window and flashed across the river. Gabriel quickly put out our lantern and we moved the boat away from the water gate to have a better look. We both stared up at the house, unsure of what we had seen. Then it happened again, the green light flashing from the window like a knife across the water.

As if we had both spoken without words, Gabriel turned the boat towards the water gate and this time we tugged as if our very lives depended on it. For a moment I thought the boat would capsize but we managed to steady it and found that we could lift the gate enough to glide under. We pushed our way in, keeping our heads low. Slap, slap, slap went the river as it hit the steps and the wall. Gabriel lit the lantern again as something slithered and flopped heavily into the water near the steps.

'Hell's bells, what was that?' said Gabriel, turning round and lifting the lantern high.

A rat sat staring at us before scurrying away.

It was hard to believe that this dark, dank place with the tidemark etched into its once white stone had ever been a place of excitement, of happy comings and goings. Now it felt abandoned and haunted, the river water swirling darkly beneath our boat.

'The sooner we find Hester, the sooner we can be out of here,' whispered Gabriel, tying the boat to a post.

We made our way up the steps towards the door that led into the house. I was surprised to find it locked. For a moment I could only think that we were to be thwarted in our plan from the outset. Then I remembered where we had always kept a spare key. I put my hand up to the ridge where one stone was hollower than the rest and there to my relief my fingers found the key.

Gabriel carefully put it in the door and turned it. It made a clunk which to us sounded as loud as thunder, and I was sure that at any moment Arise would appear before us, sword in hand. We waited with beating hearts but, hearing not a sound, opened the door and let ourselves into the dark hall.

If ever a house could feel sorry for itself it was this one, brought low by grime and neglect. It smelt musty, and it was clear that no one had swept or cleaned here since Hester had gone.

Although I had known the house all my life, it took a while for my eyes to get used to the gloom and make out the familiar shape of the hall. Suddenly, to our consternation, the study door burst open and light spilt out on to the floor. My heart near failed me for I was sure that someone had heard us and was coming to see what was going on. We stayed rooted to the spot, hardly daring to breathe, but nothing happened, no one emerged. Gabriel gave a sigh of relief, then squeezed my arm before slipping up the stairs, as quiet as a cat.

'Good mistress,' I heard a voice say from the study, 'my dear friends here may well have something you want, but they feel that they have been insufficiently paid for all the trouble they have been put to.'

'Tarbett Purman,' said a voice I recognised as Rosmore's, 'have I not brought back Maud's daughter for her, to do with as you want? Have I not given these two miserable mortals all that they desired and more over the years? All I asked for in return was the shadow. Where is it?'

I was so intent on listening that I was not aware of the noises that were coming from outside the door behind me, but in the silence that followed I could hear the click-click of claws scraping on stone steps. I began to doubt my courage as the sound grew louder and the door began to heave as if some monstrous beast was trying to break in.

I was terrified, with the kind of fear that makes everything seem like bright white light. I shut my eyes, held tightly on to my dagger, and concentrated hard on not screaming.

'It be there!' I heard Maud say.

'What is there?' said Rosmore.

'Nothing, nothing at all,' replied Arise, his voice sounding near to breaking.

'You do not deceive me, you snivelling ferret. You know what is there.'

Another flash of light came from her and through the door I saw Arise Fell fall to his knees.

'Please, no more,' he said. 'This is not my fault. You should aim your green light at Master Purman. He is the one who has ruined everything.'

'Get up, you piece of rotten flesh, and tell me what you have done with the shadow.'

Arise's voice betrayed his fear. 'I had it ready for you, but it fell into the mouth of the stuffed alligator.'

'I tried to get it back,' interrupted Tarbett Purman, 'but alas, dear madam, the alligator seemed to come to life and bit hard at my hand. I being in pain did what I could to shake it free, but sadly it fell from the window.'

'Where is it now?' she hissed.

'Down there,' said Maud, pointing to where I stood hidden in the darkness of the hall. 'It's been growing and growing, that it has. And it doesn't stop. Every day now it knocks louder on the door.'

I was sure that Rosmore would come into the hall and seek the alligator herself. Then I would be done for.

'Surely it can be got back. You have such powers,' said Maud in a trembling voice.

'No, woman,' said Rosmore, 'I cannot and I will not get it back, but you three will.'

Green light flashed across the floor and I saw Arise, Maud and Tarbett cower as the massive wings and talons of a raven swooped towards them. Cronus!

In that instant Hester and Gabriel were down the stairs. 'Quick,' said Gabriel, grabbing my arm.

'Who is there?' shouted Rosmore. 'Tarbett, go and make

sure the girl does not run away again.'

I tried to warn Gabriel not to open the door to the water gate, but everything was happening too fast. He pushed it open and beckoned us towards the steps. I could see no sign of the alligator, only the reflection of the moon on the river's surface. Hester and I scrambled into the boat and Gabriel grabbed the oars as I pushed us hard away from the steps and towards the water gate.

Too late. The raven was upon us, cawing loudly, swooping above our heads. Gabriel lifted an oar and hit out as hard as he could and we began to spin round and round. The raven flew up immediately above us, getting ready to attack. Then there was a swirl in the dark water and I saw a creamy white jaw with a mouthful of sharp pointed teeth take hold of the rope attached to our little boat.

'Sit down!' I shouted. It was just in time, for the boat took off as if we were being propelled by some wondrous machine. We all ducked low under the water gate out into the main flow of the river. The raven circled and flapped his wings but was soon left far behind.

Gabriel seized the oars. As he did so, our furious pace lessened and he soon had control of the boat. I saw the water heave and a dark shape slip back upstream.

'What in heaven's name has happened?' gasped Gabriel.

'I have no idea,' I lied. 'All that matters is that we have found Hester and she is alive and well.'

We landed the boat by the bridge just as the watch called twelve o'clock.

'That's what I like to see, a man who keeps his word! Twelve you said and twelve it is.' And with that, Master Starling patted Gabriel vigorously on the back. 'Looks as if you've done well,' he said, smiling at Hester.

'We have indeed, sir,' said Gabriel, putting an arm round Hester and smiling broadly.

We said our goodnights at the top of the steps and were about to go our separate ways when we heard a cry echo across the water.

'What was that?' I said, turning back to the river.

We stood listening.

'Oh, no doubt just some people quarrelling,' said Gabriel.

A terrible scream pierced the stillness of the night, followed by an unearthly quiet.

26

Toothmarks

*A*t high tide the river is the colour of mercury. Like an alchemist's stone it daily changes ships' cargoes into bags full of gold and silver, the wealth and prosperity of the city. With every changing tide it washes away the sins of its citizens, or so men hope and pray. For old Father Thames never judges his spoilt children who waste his riches and muddy his waters with their greed.

At each low tide the river reveals its grimy underbelly, its secrets half hidden in the sludge on its banks. Sometimes the river declines to carry its discarded passengers out to sea and they bob back up like driftwood on the surface, refusing to sink. So it was with the body of Tarbett Purman. He was found floating like a bolted cork under the piers at London Bridge, and the watermen who dragged him from the river found him with his eyes wide open and a thousand small sharp wounds in his flesh.

I was woken early. Danes, looking serious, told me to get dressed fast and come down to the kitchen. I did so, feeling sick in the pit of my stomach, for it had been late when finally we had all got to bed.

Master Thankless was up and dressed and pacing the room. Gabriel and Hester were standing holding hands.

'What is going on?' I asked, for everyone looked so solemn.

'Tarbett Purman is dead,' said Gabriel.

'Worse than dead. It is rumoured that he has been murdered,' said Master Thankless.

'Murdered? How do you know?'

'He was found floating in the river. Master Starling just came to tell us that the constable has been called. Gabriel has been accused of killing him out of jealousy and of eloping with his bride-to-be,' said Danes.

'No!' I said. 'By whom?'

'Who do you think? Arise and Maud,' said Gabriel grimly.

'But you did not do it. I was –'

'It makes no difference,' said Gabriel. 'No one is going to take the word of an apprentice over that of a preacher. I will be arrested and hanged before you can show that I am innocent.'

Hester started to cry. I wished that I was not so sleepy, for I found it hard to think straight.

'I am not having it, I tell you,' said Master Thankless. 'I am not letting them near you. Why, you are as good as a son to me. I promised your mother and father before they died that I would take care of you and I have and I will. Oddsfish, they shall not get you.' Tears rolled down the tailor's cheeks as he hugged Gabriel.

'You have been the kindest master I ever could have had,' said Gabriel. 'I am truly sorry that I have caused such trouble.'

'Trouble?' said the tailor. 'You have caused no trouble. Why, what would we have done without you? Coriander would be dead, Hester lost to us . . .'

'Captain Bailey!' I said.

They all turned to me. 'We must go to Captain Bailey. Maybe he can get Gabriel out of the city,' I said.

'An excellent idea, but alas, it will take time to find him and we have no time,' said Master Thankless.

'Master Starling could help,' I said, thinking back on the previous night and how helpful the waterman had been. 'Surely he could find Captain Bailey.'

'Yes,' said Master Thankless. 'All the same, there is no way of knowing if the Captain's ship is down at Rotherhithe or out at sea. I shall have to go and make enquiries.'

'No,' said Danes firmly. 'You must stay here and hide Gabriel. I will go, and take Hester with me. One young mistress and one old, asking after a sea captain, will look far less suspicious.'

'She's right,' said Gabriel.

'Oh dear, I am not sure,' said the tailor, looking mighty worried.

Hester went and fetched two cloaks for herself and Danes.

'Do not be vexed, Master Thankless,' she said. 'We will find Captain Bailey and he will know what to do.'

'Please take care,' said Gabriel, and he kissed her most tenderly.

'Come, we have not a moment to lose,' said Danes. 'We must get down to the river steps and find the waterman.'

*I*t seemed only minutes after their departure that there came a loud knocking and banging at the shop door.

'Open up! We have a warrant for the arrest of Gabriel Appleby.'

'Quick,' said the tailor, lifting a trapdoor in the kitchen floor. It led to steps that went down into one of the bridge piers where Master Thankless stored his cloth. Gabriel did not waste a moment and we closed the trapdoor over him, concealing it with the kitchen table and further covering it with baskets.

The bell upstairs kept on jangling, as if the Devil himself was trying to get in.

'Open this door or we will break it down!'

'There is no need for that,' said Master Thankless, rushing up the stairs to the shop and unlocking the door.

A constable marched into the shop, followed by a soldier, their boots caked with mud. They looked mighty hard men, filled with the blood of roast beef.

'Where is your apprentice Gabriel Appleby?' said the constable.

'He has gone to take some gowns to a customer. Why? What is this all about?'

The constable shoved a paper into Master Thankless's

hands. 'The breaking of the sixth commandment. Murder, that's what!' He clattered up the stairs to our chambers, leaving the soldier to look round the shop.

'Whose gown is this?' asked the soldier, picking up a dress that the tailor had nearly finished.

'It has been made for a humble and godly lady,' said Master Thankless.

The soldier ripped off the sleeves. 'The Apostle Paul would have us fashion ourselves for God, not for the world. This is unseemly, a garment not befitting a devout woman,' he said. With that he tore the bodice apart, pulling from it all its fine trimmings.

'Please leave it,' begged the tailor.

'Clothes for strumpets,' said a soldier, stabbing at the skirt with his knife. 'A woman should be plainly dressed so that a man can keep his mind on God.'

'Look at this,' said the constable, dragging Nell down the stairs. 'She was hiding under the bed. Who is she?'

'I am maid to Master Thankless,' said Nell.

'Where is Gabriel Appleby?'

'On my honour, sir, I do not know,' said Nell.

'You know what happens to girls who lie,' said the constable, picking up an empty glass and letting it smash in front of Nell. She crossed her arms and looked very put out to be spoken to in such a tone.

'Come, let us look in the kitchen,' said the constable, and he and the soldier tramped downstairs and started with much delight to pull the kitchen to pieces.

'Still don't know where your apprentice is?' asked the constable.

'No,' said Master Thankless.

The constable went over to the fireplace, taking from it a tankard given to Master Thankless by a customer before the Civil War. Slowly he read out the inscription. '*A Gift from Lord Selbury*. Now why do I know that name? Of course. I never forget a good hanging. If I remember rightly he was the Royalist supporter who took to being a highwayman after his lands were confiscated by our great leader Oliver Cromwell.' He threw the tankard on to the floor and lifted his boot high above it. 'Are you sure you don't know where your apprentice is?'

Master Thankless, with sweat running from his forehead, said, 'No.' And the boot came down hard and the tankard lay twisted and broken.

The constable came up close to Master Thankless's face and almost spat the words at him.

'You know the penalty for perjury. You will be taken to join your apprentice on the gallows.'

Master Thankless said nothing.

'What's all this?' said the soldier, pushing away the kitchen table, and he kicked the baskets across the room so that the trapdoor was revealed.

'It is a storeroom where I keep my cloth,' said the tailor.

'Open it!' ordered the constable.

Master Thankless slowly lifted the heavy door. The soldier

pushed him out of the way and climbed down to the first rung of the ladder.

Suddenly there came a cry from the shop and another soldier burst into the kitchen. 'Come quick! He has been spotted on Bridge Street, running towards the City.'

In an instant the soldier climbed back up the ladder and pushed past the tailor and up the stairs, followed by the constable. He slammed the shop door so hard that the front of the shop shook.

The sense of relief was mighty. None of us dared say a word until the hubbub in the street had calmed down. Master Thankless, Nell and I stood in the chaos of the kitchen looking down through the trapdoor until Gabriel poked his head out. He saw the wrecked kitchen and the broken tankard. 'What have I brought upon you?' he cried.

'Nothing that cannot be mended and made whole,' said Master Thankless. 'Though no one in this fair city can mend a hanged man. Come, let us hide you in the attic.'

'Pigs, that's what I call them. Worse than pigs' turds,' said Nell. 'Look what they've gone and done.' She started picking up the broken crockery. 'Brought half the filth from the street and smeared it everywhere. Worse than turdy toads.'

'Hush, Nell!' I said, trying not to laugh.

'I hate them,' she said. 'I wish we had the King back. Anything rather than old Noll and his henchmen.'

We spent the rest of that day tidying up, terrified in case the Constable returned. It was not until nightfall that the bell rang softly and Danes, Hester and Captain Bailey slipped into the darkened shop and down to the kitchen.

'Where is Gabriel?' said Hester, taking off her cloak.

'Safe,' I said. 'He is upstairs in the attic. Come with me.' I went with her only as far as the attic steps, for Gabriel had heard her and come down. She rushed to him so I thought best to leave them and went back down to the kitchen.

'What has been going on here?' said Danes, looking at Nell, who had a bucket in her hand and strands of hair falling over her face.

'The constable and his soldier, that's what,' said Nell. 'Tried to tear the house down, they did. Smashed everything they found. They're revolting, them Roundheads.'

'Oh, am I pleased to see you, good captain!' said the tailor. 'I am in fear of my life if those two come back.'

'Then we are not a moment too soon,' said Captain Bailey.

Gabriel and Hester came into the room.

'I never murdered anyone, sir,' said Gabriel, who in the space of a day had aged beyond his years with worry.

'And I believe you, lad,' said Captain Bailey. 'Well, we should be making a move. Get your cloak and hat. I am sailing for France on the next good tide. What say you to that?'

'I want Hester to come too, sir,' was Gabriel's reply.

'No, lad,' laughed the sea captain good-heartedly. 'I will take you. Alone.'

'Then I will not go,' said Gabriel. 'I cannot leave Hester. She is my life.'

The smile disappeared from Captain Bailey's face.

'What say you, Hester?' he asked.

'I do not want to be parted from Gabriel. I love him with all my heart.'

'Well, here's a salty barrel of eels,' said the Captain, looking at the tailor.

It was Danes who spoke. 'The constable will be looking for Gabriel alone. It would be safer for them to leave together and travel as husband and wife. And Hester could not be without Gabriel. She would pine her life away.'

'I agree with Mistress Danes,' said Master Thankless. 'Better if she is away from here, for the constable will surely take her back to Thames Street if he finds her.'

'Then do not say another word,' said the sea captain. 'Come, both of you. Let us be gone and I will see to it that you are married.'

I had never seen Hester look happier and I have never seen a young man look more pleased. Whatever their future held, at least they had each other.

'Here,' said Master Thankless, and he handed Gabriel a bag of coins. 'This should help you.'

'I cannot take your money, master,' said Gabriel.

'You can and you will. And I want you both to come home again when all this has been sorted out. Do you understand? You are free now, a journeyman.'

Master Thankless went with them, lantern in hand, to make sure they found their way to the end of the bridge, for a thick fog had come down which all agreed was the best cover for their escape. We watched them go and felt mighty pleased when Master Thankless returned, saying they had got away with the ferryman and by now should be past the Tower of London.

We had no more visits from the constable or his soldiers. There were many who swore they had seen Gabriel, either in the City or down by the old Globe, and a notice went up to say that Gabriel Appleby, an apprentice from Bridge Street, was a wanted man.

That was not the end of it. Master Thankless was determined to get the charges against Gabriel dropped and both Danes and he filled the empty shop with that hope.

The sheriff had called in a searcher, a Mistress Parfitt. It always strikes me as a miserable job to have to go round and see how people died, but Mistress Parfitt was known to be good at it and her word much respected. She said she did not believe that Tarbett Purman had been knifed, but instead was the victim of some dreadful accident. As a result, his body was not released for burial, which Danes and Master Thankless took to be a good sign.

The plague had ceased to have its hold over the city. People had begun to return from the countryside, hungry for gossip. Tarbett Purman's strange and untimely death held a great fascination for many. Among them was an eminent apothecary who requested to see the body, even though the smell from it must, I thought, by now be most putrid and unpleasant. He pronounced that the marks on Tarbett Purman could not have been brought about either by dagger or by knife. They were wounds that belonged more to the animal kingdom than the realm of man. He added darkly that in his personal opinion it was the work of the Devil and proof, if ever proof was needed, that he stalked the earth.

The alligator was no devil. I knew one who was, though, and he went by the name of Arise Fell.

27
The Invisible Rope

I have thought a lot about skirts and how they make the world that much smaller for women. Uncluttered by petticoats, unencumbered by aprons which bind a woman to house and home, in breeches a man can all but fly. In truth, I had been much disappointed, for I had hoped for a chance to find the shadow when I went to Thames Street with Gabriel. I yearned to be a boy again, for I could think of no other way to get back into my house.

It had been a week now since Gabriel and Hester had gone, and every night I dreamt the same dream. The hounds were chasing me and I had to run for my life. The ground was white, thick snow was falling, and the forest trees were bare and black. The fox raced beside me, looking at me with his brown eyes. The dogs and huntsmen were still at our heels. I could only see the great white horse when its form was outlined against the dark night. I felt the breath of the hounds and thought my end had come.

The dogs were on me and over me. Their teeth were bare

and saliva dripped from their snarling mouths. But then I realised it was not me they were after. They surrounded the fox, their tongues hanging out. They were going in for the kill. The huntsman's horn rang out across the fields and I could see blood seep into the snow.

I woke and knew that I could wait no longer by this world's hourglass. I must find the shadow and save Tycho.

I could not tell Master Thankless or Danes of my plans, for they were already worried enough about Gabriel and Hester. I felt very bad to think that I would be making matters worse for them by disappearing.

All through that long dull day I went over my plans again and again.

'You are as fidgety as a blanket of fleas,' said Danes to me as we folded fabric in the shop.

I wanted to tell her everything as I always had but all I could say was 'When the King comes back then all will be well.'

'I am sure you are right,' said Danes, 'though when that will be I do not know, for that old tyrant is still a healthy man and a king in all but name. I think he will keep us under his iron claw a while longer.'

I could think of nothing to say, anxious that more words might betray me. To tell the truth, I was terrified that this could be my last day on this earth, the last time I would see my beloved Danes and Master Thankless, and I fought back tears.

'Is something ailing you?' Danes asked.

'No,' I said, 'nothing that a hug would not put right.'

There is a smell to Danes of fresh bread and lavender, a smell that says home to me, and I wanted to remember it, take it with me like a nosegay.

As we were laying the table for supper Master Thankless rushed into the kitchen.

'Master Starling came by just as I was closing the shop to tell me that Hester and Gabriel have landed safely in La Rochelle,' he said, taking Danes's hand and dancing her round the kitchen. 'A toast to a safe arrival!' And he brought out his finest brandy.

I did my best to appear cheerful, though my hands felt as cold as my feet and the brandy tasted bitter as guilt. I hated to think what they would be saying tomorrow after I had gone. This thought worried me much and so I wrote a note and left it on my bed for Master Thankless to read to Danes in the morning. I hoped that it would comfort them.

When everyone had gone to bed I dressed once more in the clothes of a young lad and wrapped up my silver shoes and put them away inside my doublet. I was taking them with me in the hope that somehow they would allow me back into my mother's kingdom.

Finally, when the watchman called in midnight, I went softly down the stairs. All was quiet, all heavy with that yeasty smell of sleep. I looked round the shop once more before letting myself out, and thought that this would still be here after I was gone, and it made me feel braver to think of it.

I was glad of the moon for my house lay in utter darkness. No lantern was lit outside. The sign of the mulberry tree that once had swung proud over the gate was now faded, the paint peeling.

I wrapped my cloak around me and looked up and down the street to make sure that no one was around. There is a way of opening the garden gate without a key. I had watched Danes do it many times and when I was small would try it myself, though then I did not have the strength needed. Tonight it was easy. I slipped my index finger into the lock and, pulling back the catch, opened the gate. In the moonlight the garden looked dry and tired, withered from lack of water and care.

All was deadly still as I made my way into the house. The hall, as on my last visit, was unlit. In the gloom I could make out a higgledy-piggledy tower of tables and chairs, piled up against the door that led to the water gate. I wondered if this strange maypole was intended to keep out the alligator, for I could see no other reason for it. Then I felt a small pudgy hand grab me from behind.

'I got her, Arise,' Maud shouted up the stairs. 'She's dressed as a boy, but I smelt her out.' There was no answer. 'Arise!' she shrieked. 'Do you hear me? She's come, just as you said she would.'

I pulled my arm free.

'Not so fast,' she said. 'You shall not get away this time.'

She looked quite wild, her eyes opened wide. She wore no cap. Instead, her long thin hair hung down in greasy rat's tails so that patches of her bald skull could be seen. Her breath smelled of rancid butter and her clothes looked unwashed.

Suddenly a light shone from the top of the stairs and there stood Arise holding a lantern, the light of which was reflected in his insect green glasses.

'Ann,' he said, 'you have come back to us.'

Just for one moment I felt my old fear of him, but I took all my courage and said, 'Ann? That is not my name and you know it.'

'How dare you talk so to a man of God!' said Maud, striking out at me. I saw her doing it and nearly let myself be a child again. Then I heard a voice in my head say calmly, 'You are taller than she, you are a grown woman. You can stop this.'

I pushed her hard away and said, 'You touch me, Maud Jarret, and you will much regret it.' My voice sounded strong, stronger than I felt.

To my surprise she backed away.

'Arise,' she said, 'kill her so that at least we have something to show –'

'Quiet, woman,' said Arise, walking down the stairs towards me. I stood as tall as I could. I would rather die, I thought, than flinch from this crooked man. He came near, smelling much of drink, and I comforted myself by thinking he was not as tall as I remembered. 'What have you come for?' he asked.

'The same thing you seek,' I replied.

'And what might that be?' he said mockingly.

'Fairy silver,' I replied.

'Do not listen to her,' said Maud. 'She is the Devil, trying to trick us.'

'No I am not,' I said, and I said it clear. I said it for Hester, for Joan and for Danes. I said it for my father and I said it for me, Coriander.

'It is you who have been listening to the Devil's words. It is you who have murdered and deceived in the name of your own greed.'

Arise laughed, a hollow unpleasant laugh, and lifted his hand.

I stood firm. I said, 'You are the only devil here.'

At that moment the pile of furniture gave a lurch and fell crashing to the floor. The river door swung open. Arise's hand dropped to his side and he took several steps back towards the stairs and held on to the banister. For out of the muddle of tables and chairs came the snout of a monstrous large alligator. I stayed where I was as Maud rushed to Arise and clung to him, begging him to do something.

He brought his hand of wrath hard down on her. Still she would not let go.

'Save me!' she screamed, but the hand of salvation still held tight to the lantern that swung back and forth, light and dark across their terrified faces.

I looked at them both standing there and felt such loathing. I knew that I had nothing to fear from the alligator. He came into the hall and stopped by my side as if he had been looking for me.

'Go on then,' shouted Arise. 'Kill her, kill her like you did Tarbett Purman.'

The alligator slowly turned his head towards me. I knew

what he was thinking and I nodded. The beast moved with great speed towards the stairs.

Maud pushed Arise down in her haste to get past him and safely out of reach on the first landing.

'No!' shouted Arise. 'The girl!' He pointed a long-nailed finger in my direction. The alligator advanced towards him. I followed.

The alligator took hold of his ankle.

Arise let out a terrifying scream and tried hard to pull his leg away. 'Come here and help me!' he shouted up the stairs.

The alligator let go. Arise's stockings were soaked with blood. He hobbled up the stairs and, pushing past Maud, made for my father's old bedchamber, where he fumbled desperately for his ring of keys. Maud lurched after him, but Arise closed the door in her face and locked it.

'Let me in!' shouted Maud, banging her fists on the door.

'No, woman,' said Arise. 'I care not what happens to you.'

Maud turned to me and whimpered, 'Rosmore will be here any moment and that will be the end of both of you.'

The alligator slithered towards her. Maud stood frozen on the landing.

It only took one knock from the alligator's scaly claws for the door to give way. The bedchamber was empty save for the lantern. Arise had climbed up on to the windowsill, his hand of wrath out before him, the hand of salvation holding on to the window latch.

'Stay away from me, you fairy child. Stay away!'

'What is my name?' I said.

'Ann,' he said.

The alligator opened his jaw. His teeth glimmered in the moonlight, sharp as knives.

'What is my name?' I said again.

'Coriander,' screamed Arise, letting the ring of keys fall to the floor. He pushed back hard against the fretted glass that cracked under his weight. With a splintering sound the window gave way and the preacher fell into the river below.

I ran to the window and looked down. There was nothing to see in the dark river water. I hoped with all my heart that that was the last of the preacher.

I picked up the lantern and the keys, following the alligator back down the stairs towards the study. I unlocked the door. The room was completely bare like the bedchamber above it.

The alligator stood in front of the ebony cabinet and once more opened his enormous jaws. I looked at those sharp teeth, that creamy mouth, and I remembered well the time when I had put my hand inside to get the key to open the cabinet so that I could wear a pair of silver shoes.

I knew what I had to do. I knelt down and as the lantern light flickered then waned, I felt the sharp wind of the raven's wings as it flew into the room, followed by Rosmore. I stood up. The alligator shut his mouth tight.

'Well, Coriander, we meet again.' She was dressed in a long dusty cloak that looked as if it was made of spiders' webs. Her face was cruel and sharp. Cronus landed on her outstretched arm.

'Well, my beauty, what have we here?'

'A princess, no less,' the raven answered.

'Who does this princess resemble?' she asked.

'Why,' said the raven, 'Princess Eleanor, your stepdaughter.'

'Oh clever bird,' she whispered. 'And tell me, what thought I of Princess Eleanor?'

'That she disobeyed you to run away with a mere human.'

'Ah,' she said, 'it saddens me to remember it. But now the wrong she did can be put right through the daughter. Come, girl, give me what is mine.'

While she was speaking, half to the raven, half to me, I had been watching a figure behind her. Like some giant rat emerging from the door that led to the river came the wet and watery figure of Arise, his green glasses gone, his pale eyes the colour of fish scales.

The raven let out a loud squawk as Rosmore spun round. Arise fell to his knees as green light flashed from her hands.

'You failed to keep your promise,' said Rosmore. 'Avarice and greed overcame you.'

'I was not to know that being in the chest would not kill her.'

'You fool!' she laughed. 'You displeased me at your peril. You thought that you were clever enough to outwit a Fairy Queen. I warned you not to meddle in things you did not understand.'

Another flash of green light snaked across towards him, lifting him off his feet to spin round and round in the air, river water dripping from his black shiny coat.

Maud tried to slip away and creep up the stairs to the attic. Seeing her Rosmore laughed again.

'No, please,' whimpered Maud, 'not me.'

It was then that the alligator opened his mouth to smile. I knelt down and quickly pulled through his teeth the silver gossamer of my mother's shadow.

'Good girl,' said Rosmore, seeing what I held in my hands.

'Let him down,' pleaded Maud, coming closer to Rosmore and pulling at her spidery cloak. 'We do not deserve this. Let him down and we will both be gone.'

'Quiet,' commanded Rosmore. 'I am not to be played with. I told you what would happen if you disobeyed me.'

'All I wish is that you do not break his bones,' said Maud again.

'Another wish! Oh, what a pleasure! Have I not told you to be careful what you wish for?' Rosmore laughed again. 'It might just happen. You want the crooked man's bones unbroken? You may have them.'

'No,' shouted Arise. 'She does not wish it.'

Green light danced from Rosmore's hand, looping and coiling, up to where Arise hung suspended. His hands grabbed the rope of light and then he fell as if he were in the hangman's noose at Tyburn, his body twitching and twisting in space. At last he was still.

I knew that Arise Fell was truly dead.

Maud screamed and screamed.

'Silence, you babbling jade,' shouted Rosmore, 'silence, unless you want to join him.'

Maud stood looking at the pile of bones on the floor and stuffed her chubby hands in her mouth.

Rosmore turned to me and whispered to Cronus, 'Tell her, my beauty, tell her to give it to me. Tell her.'

I looked at the shadow in my hands and watched as the silver sank into my skin and disappeared. I saw the raven slowly flap his broad wings and I saw a tiny stuffed alligator sitting on the floor.

I said, though my voice seemed to come from far away, 'This is my mother's shadow. It belongs to me.'

The room began to fade, Rosmore becoming a thin veil. Her voice was all I could hear. She hissed, 'I will kill you. There will be no escaping.'

Her words trailed away and then she was gone. I felt as a bird in flight must do when looking at a city from a great height, as first the house on Thames Street and then London itself disappeared and I knew where I was.

And so the fifth part of my tale is told, and with it another candle goes out.

PART SIX

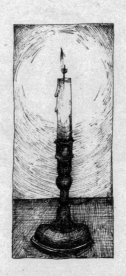

28

The Night of the Fox

I found myself alone in a forest, snow falling, the light shining an eerie blue through the darkening trees. This place I knew all too well. I had dreamt of it often since I had been back on Bridge Street. This was where they killed the fox.

I heard a huntsman's horn ring out and I started to run. I was in my nightmare but this time I knew there was to be no waking.

Oh, how I ran. I slipped, I stumbled, I fell, got up again and carried on until, exhausted, I could go no further. My breath rose like steam from a cooking pot. I stood frozen with fear, my eyes shut, hoping that I was only a blue light, knowing in my heart that I was not.

I shuddered with fright as I felt a horse's hot breath on my neck. Terrified, I opened my eyes to see Tycho's white stallion standing behind me. The sense of relief was overwhelming but short-lived.

The cries of the huntsmen rang out again, the noise darting from tree to tree, echoing through the frozen forest. Were they behind me or in front of me? Without another thought I grasped the horse's silvery mane and with much difficulty pulled myself up on to his back. In truth, I had never been on a horse before and I felt certain that I would fall. As if sensing my anxiety, he slowed down until I had the rhythm of him and only then did he set off at an almighty gallop. I held on for all I was worth.

We galloped out of the forest and over fields bordered with hedges of holly and looking like pieces of Danes's needlework. My cap came off my head and my hair blew out in the wind. I allowed myself to glance back once to see in the distance the misty outline of the huntsmen.

We rode on without stopping until at last the white horse came to rest at the top of a hill. From here I could view the valley below. Silhouetted above the snow-filled trees stood a tower. Nearby I could see several small hamlets, hugging the dips in the landscape. Smoke curled up from their chimneys. What would I not give now to be sitting by a fire somewhere safe and warm?

Night was beginning to draw in, the moon a watery tear in the sky. The cold had crept into my bones. Snowflakes whirled into my face, and my fingers were numb. I started as I saw a black carriage driven by four black horses, a slash across the white winter landscape, make its way towards the tower. The sight made me feel sick. Rosmore was near. The white horse, as if sensing my terror, moved swiftly into the cover of the silvery trees that gave way to a wild tangled wood. I could hear the howl of wolves and the hoot of an owl and I buried my head in the horse's soft mane, comforting myself with his warmth, his smell.

The horse stopped at a tumbledown hut. He pawed urgently at the ground. I slithered down and stood staring at the unwelcoming place. Seeing my hesitation, the horse nuzzled me forward as an icy wind whipped up a flurry of snow. The cold was now so intense that my teeth began to chatter. I was shivering so much that I could not feel my hands as I opened the latch. I stood in the doorway, unable to see anything.

'Is anyone there?' I called to the darkness, and nearly jumped out of my skin when I heard a low moan in reply.

'Who is it?' I whispered.

The moon shone in, as if curious to know the answer, and by her watery light I could see the wounded fox, an arrow in his side, blood seeping on to the wooden floor.

'No!' I cried. 'Please no! Let it not be so.'

I knelt down beside the fox and held his paw. I had come too late. The fox was dying, his dark eyes cloudy. I stroked his fur, tears rolling down my face, and felt as if I was drowning in sorrow. I knew that, like Tycho, I too would be hunted and killed by Rosmore.

For what? A shadow whose power I did not understand. Should I lie down like a lamb and die with the fox? I felt close to despair. What was the point in going on? I sobbed, silvery tears rolling down my cheeks on to his bloodsoaked fur. I was overcome with grief for all that I had lost, all that should have been.

I woke with a start, unsure of what had happened. I was lying curled up on the floor, a fur pulled over me. A wintry morning light shone through the broken shutters and snow was blowing into the empty hut. I could not see the body of the fox anywhere, only a scattering of tiny animal bones. If he had died in the night surely he would be here? Yet there was nothing.

Had it all been a dream? What could have happened? Where was the fox? Where was the white horse? I felt very frightened and very alone.

Stiff with cold, I got up so suddenly that the little hut began to spin. I put out a hand to steady myself on a wooden shelf. Down in the grate a feeble fire was stuttering to life. Who had lit it? The arrow that last night I was sure had been in the fox's side was leaning against a pile of firewood.

I was pulled up short when I stared at the dusty shelf. I wondered if my eyes played tricks with me, for there lay the most wondrous and delicate gold locket, embroidered with diamonds. What such riches were doing here abandoned I had no idea. Who could have left such a locket?

'I knew you would come,' I heard a voice behind me say softly. 'I knew that one day I would see you, that you would come back and save me.'

I spun round and there, standing in the doorway, was a young man who looked as wild as any animal, his hair long and with a beard that covered nearly all his face. His clothes hung from his thin bony body as if they belonged to someone else.

'Coriander, your disguise does not fool me. Do you not know me?' he said.

I looked at him. That voice I recognised, those brown eyes I knew. 'Tycho?' I said, though I had no faith in my words.

'Yes,' he said, coming into the room. He moved as if his body was a stranger to him.

'I do not understand,' I said. 'Last night you were a wounded fox, an arrow in your side.'

'Coriander, I have been a fox since I refused to marry Unwin. It was Rosmore's curse. I took refuge here in Medlar's hut.'

'Medlar?' I said. 'So you know him well?'

'Very well,' said Tycho. 'Medlar gave me hope, for he was certain that you would come back with the shadow. Every day with this hope in my heart I fought to stay alive, wondering and waiting.'

'I wish I could have got here sooner, but it was not to be,' I said.

'I watched you sleep, and wondered how your silvery tears had made me well. I can only think that you have brought the shadow back. Am I right?'

I nodded.

'I thank you,' said Tycho, and he moved forward to touch me. I backed away. 'Forgive me,' he said, hanging his head. 'I disgust you like this.'

'No,' I said. 'No, but I am shocked to see you so. I thought that if I were to bring back the shadow, all would be well.'

'Only when Rosmore is gone will the spell be truly broken.'

I felt ashamed of my reaction. It was true he did not look the same, but he was still the person I remembered, and I thought of all he had been through and how abandoned and alone he must have felt out here, with only the white horse for company.

He went over to the shelf and tentatively picked up the gold locket and opened it. Sweet music filled the hut, gentle as a lullaby. It sounded strange in this cold and lonely place, and I was reminded of my mother and of our home in Thames Street before my world was shattered.

'Here,' said Tycho, showing me a tiny painting that lay like a thumbprint in the gold locket. 'This is a portrait of you. It does not do you justice. You are far more beautiful. Your eyes are river-green.'

'But where did you get it? How did anyone know what I looked like?'

'Medlar followed you back. He has his ways.'

I went over to him and took both his hands. 'With all my heart I am pleased to see you,' I said.

He turned and looked at me. 'I have thought of you every day since we last met.'

'So have I, and I have often wished that I might see you again,' I said, blushing.

'Though not like this,' he added with a laugh.

'Rosmore is back,' I said. 'Last night I saw her carriage.'

'Then we must be gone from here,' he said.

He went towards the door of the hut and sent out a long, low whistle.

Nothing happened. No white horse appeared. He called again. Across the snowy fields all was deadly still. Even the wind seemed frozen in its tracks. Something was wrong.

'Coriander!' shouted Tycho. He slammed the door and rushed back towards me, pulling me to the floor. As he did so, the raven flew in at the shuttered window, splintering it to pieces, and swooped down on us, his claws outstretched. Tycho rolled over on top of me as Cronus came at us again, claws tearing at Tycho's doublet. Tycho hit out at the bird with his bare hands. Then, with a sweep of wings, the raven was gone.

'You are hurt,' I said, and I touched his arm. A silvery gossamer light came from my fingers and the wound was gone. I could feel my heart beating. I was scared. I was truly scared.

'What is happening?' I asked.

'You must not be afraid, Coriander,' said Tycho. 'The shadow is yours to keep. It is within you and cannot be taken from you unless you let it.'

He picked up a stick and opened the door a crack.

'What are you going to do?'

'We will make a run for it.'

'No,' I said, pulling him back. 'Look!'

I stared at the fire and saw the flames stand upright in the grate like a painted picture. I remembered seeing that once before, when I first met Rosmore on London Bridge. I was sure that she was nearby.

Tycho pulled the door to and went cautiously to the window. Outside we could hear the snorting and neighing of many huntsmen's horses.

'Think you can escape? Think again,' crowed the raven above the now deafening noise of the barking dogs.

We sat hunched against the wall of the hut, Tycho still holding the stick.

'Come out or we will set the dogs on you,' screeched Cronus.

Tycho looked at me, his eyes wild with anger. I held tight to him, fearful that he might do something foolhardy. Standing in the doorway stood two huge huntsmen. There was no escape. Tycho got up and rushed at them, trying to protect me. They hit out at him and threw him hard across the room.

I ran to where he fell and touched his face. Once again, I saw the light dart from me to him. He pulled himself to his feet.

'What are you doing here?' he shouted, throwing himself in front of me.

'We have no interest in you,' said one of the huntsmen coldly. 'It is the girl we want. Now move away before I kill you.'

'Please, Tycho,' I cried, 'do as they say.'

The huntsman pushed him away but still Tycho would not give up, not until the huntsman had him tight in his grasp. The other one picked me up as if I were no more than a rag doll.

'What shall we do with him?' said the huntsman, giving Tycho a blow in the side.

'Bring him,' said my captor. 'When he has changed back to a fox we can have more sport.'

29

The Light of Shadows

It must have been around midday when we finally arrived at the tower. It was dark and forbidding, a place where the sun would be shy of shining, and I recognised it from my mother's painting. A feeling of cold terror settled on me.

The tower was tall, very tall, built from black stone with no windows. The land around it was bare. Even the trees kept their distance, for nothing grew in this frozen place.

The huntsmen and their dogs surrounded the tower. They dragged Tycho to one side and tethered him to a stake. I was led roughly to the door of the tower.

'No,' shouted Tycho, fighting like a wild animal to pull himself free. 'Leave her be. Take me, not her. Leave her!'

The huntsman cracked his whip. 'Quiet, fox,' he shouted, pushing me inside and closing the door behind me.

The silence in this dark, damp place was overwhelming, and I felt as if the stone walls were sucking all warmth from me. An unnatural green light hung in the air, illuminating the stairs that looked worn down by many feet. I was sure that whoever had climbed up here had done so, like me, with a heavy heart and an even heavier tread.

At the top there was an oak door that creaked open as if it had been waiting for me. I found myself in a room that was triangular in shape, the ceiling going up to a sharp point. It was made entirely of small panes of green glass. I felt as though I were deep underwater.

Rosmore was seated in an ornate chair, the sides of which were carved like huge wooden wings. She looked like some strange flightless bird, dressed in a dark purple gown with a shawl of ravens' feathers. In her hand she held her mirror and at her side sat the raven on his perch, watching me.

I stood still, trying to catch my breath. I was shivering with cold and fright and so weak with hunger that my eyes began to play tricks, for it seemed to me as though there were endless Rosmores, one behind the other, going on into infinity.

'I have waited too long for this day,' she said, stroking the raven's head. 'Have I not, my beauty?'

'Too long,' echoed Cronus.

'What have I to do with all this?' I said, my legs shaking.

Rosmore laughed, her face, sharp as a knife, coming into focus as she leant towards me.

'What indeed? Did your mother never tell you? Shall I tell you?'

'Oh do,' cawed the raven harshly.

'It was like this, Coriander. Many years ago, long before you were born, I heard that your grandfather King Nablus had had a daughter, born with a shadow made of everlasting light. Oh Cronus, Coriander is baffled! Do you know how rare such a shadow is? It is the most precious gift a fairy can ever be given, and I knew that it was meant for me, not some wretched, snivelling child who would never understand the meaning of it.'

'I still do not understand,' I said.

'That surprises me not,' said Rosmore. 'You are your mother's child, I see. The shadow holds beauty. It holds life itself. It holds power, untold power. With it, I will rule this world.'

'Quite,' said Cronus, 'and we devised a plan. You took a present to King Nablus's wife. Alas, within a week she was dead.'

Rosmore put her hands to her heart. 'Such a pity!' she said.

I backed away from her. I had a sudden memory of the day my mother was taken ill, the way she fell, the pearls dancing on the floor, the raven's wings shattering the glass. Cronus! I gasped as if I had been punched. Rosmore was responsible not only for the death of my grandmother but of my mother as well.

'Your poor grandfather, left alone with his newborn child, was heartbroken. It was not hard to persuade the grieving King to marry me, to let me take his daughter Eleanor under my wing.' She laughed. 'How sweet and sensitive she was. Oh, how I enjoyed making her life a misery! I made sure the King was spellbound and saw nothing amiss.'

Rosmore held up the mirror and turned it towards me. As

she did so, I fell to my knees, clutching at my stomach.

'How could you be so cruel!' I said.

It felt as if an invisible hand was pulling at my insides, and to my horror I saw coming from me a wisp of the silver shadow, attracted by the dark glass of the mirror. It hung in the air, suspended between us. Rosmore held her mirror closer.

'Stupid girl! I bided my time, had this mirror made to catch the shadow in, waited until Eleanor was your age. She thought she had tricked me and got away, but this time the shadow will be mine. You will not be able to hold on. You are a fool even to try.' And she drummed her fingers on the arm of the chair. 'But if you want to suffer, no matter. I have waited so long for this that a little longer makes no difference.'

'What are you doing?' I gasped. I was in such agony, feeling the shadow dragged from me.

'Taking back what is rightfully mine.'

I thought to keep her talking, for I found the pain was less as long as she spoke.

'A child's shadow is a fickle thing. The shadow needed to be full grown to have its power. I arranged that your mother should marry and I planned to steal it on her wedding night.'

I felt myself getting weaker, but I managed to say, 'What kept you?'

Rosmore stopped drumming her nails and leant forward, her face twisted with anger.

'Eleanor, Eleanor. I grew sick of hearing her name. She

thought to outwit me. Married a mortal, went to London, grew a garden, healed the sick!' she sneered. 'And much good it did her. She was seen as a witch, a cunning woman. She met the end she deserved.'

'You killed her!' I yelled.

'What if I did? Your mother thought that she could keep the shadow from me. She hid it in a lead-lined casket so that I could not find it. Clever, for we cannot see through lead.'

'Let me go,' I cried.

'No. You shall die, just like your mother, but first the shadow will be mine. Do you want to know how I found you?'

'No!' I screamed.

'Medlar,' continued Rosmore. 'Medlar told the King he had a granddaughter. Cronus heard him, didn't you, my beauty?'

'I did,' said the raven.

'The King ordered a pair of silver shoes to be made for his little princess.'

'What?' I cried. 'It was the King?'

'Your grandfather. You know who you are. Do you think I would be bothered with a mere mortal? I put a curse on them. I came to visit you on London Bridge. I was curious to know what Eleanor's daughter would be like. You took after your mother. A weakling, a butterfly to be broken, a mouse to be played with.'

All the time she was speaking I was doing my best to hold the shadow in me. I dreaded her pulling any harder, for I was sure that I would die.

'Let go,' she ordered. 'Let go. It will be better for you if you do.'

I was lying curled up in torment when I heard the voice of my mother saying, gently and calmly, like cool water after great thirst, 'Coriander, you still have the shadow. Hold fast. She cannot take it from you unless you let her.'

I lifted my head and looked at Rosmore. I saw her mouth like an open wound, but I could hear no sound. I knew not what she was, but I hated her for killing my mother, for ruining our happiness, for her miserable greed.

The more I thought like this the more the pain lifted, and I found that I was able to stand up. As I did so, the silver light began to be absorbed into my skin again.

Rosmore came closer.

'Do not dare,' she said, holding the dark glass before her.

'The mirror, Coriander,' said my mother's voice, 'the mirror.'

Feeling braver, I put out my hands to take it. Silver light shot from my fingertips and then, in one swift movement, I snatched the mirror from Rosmore and the shadow sank once again back into my skin.

Now I had the power I needed and without question I knew what I must do. I turned the mirror towards Rosmore. She started but quickly collected herself.

'Do you think you can outwit me? I will show you. Snuff out the day,' she commanded. 'Let the prince become a fox again.' She raised her hand and immediately the sky darkened and became as black as night.

The raven took off from his perch, circling higher and higher up to the point of the glass roof. Then he swooped down on me. I put my hands up to push him away and at once I saw the shadow spin from me and catch the raven, bringing him down hard on the stone floor.

'Cronus my beauty,' cried Rosmore. She turned back to me. 'You cursed girl. I'll kill you for that.'

Time seemed to slow down. I could hear Rosmore screeching. I could see the raven, one wing spread, hobbling along the floor. I knew what to do. I allowed myself to feel all the anger, all the misery, and all the grief for everything that had happened to me. It was like a tight knotted ball and it came to the surface, passed through to the mirror and like an arrow shot from a bow went straight for Rosmore.

She cried out as it struck her, throwing her hard against the green glass walls as they cracked open to let in gusts of frozen air.

'No!' she raged, pushing her hands out before her, trying with all her might to resist the ball of silver light. I stood my ground. I believed in my strength. I flicked my fingers and again light burst from me.

She gave a piercing scream as she fell through the broken glass, searching desperately for wings that were not there. I ran to the shattered wall to see her plummet to the ground and explode like a giant firework, sending out sparks of light that whirled and whizzed before fading away.

The horses reared up in terror as Rosmore's spell was finally broken, and before my eyes the huntsmen and their dogs were transformed into ravens that flew up towards the sky to chase the inky tail of night. I let the mirror drop and saw its liquid spill out on to the floor.

As I ran for the stairs, Cronus flapped his wings, uncertain of flight, and then with a lopsided gait took off and flew out and away through the broken glass.

30

Bittersweet

I heard Tycho call my name. I ran down the stairs two at a time, so thrilled was I to see him. It almost took my breath away to see how handsome he was.

'Coriander, the spell is truly broken,' he said jubilantly. 'I am myself again. Everything now will be restored to the way it was. Rosmore is dead. Look, spring is no longer waiting in the wings, longing for its entrance. It is centre stage. This is only the beginning. This is the restoration.' He lifted me up in the air and we spun round.

The white horse came and nuzzled Tycho's neck. He laughed, and stroking the horse's mane said, 'We both think you brave.'

'There is still much I do not understand,' I said. 'Why did my mother not know the power of the shadow? It could have saved her.'

Tycho sighed. 'Medlar told me that she had been so crushed by Rosmore that she saw it only as a terrible burden. She did not want it, and neither did she want Rosmore to have it, knowing too well her nature. Your mother wanted to be free of the shadow altogether.'

'It has sunk into my skin,' I said.

Tycho put his arms round me. 'It was meant for you, I am sure of that.'

I rested my head against him. 'Now what?' I said.

'Come home with me. Let me show you my city. It has a river that runs as green as opal through it.'

'And,' I whispered, 'it has mermaids and mermen that push boats from one side to the other. There is a bridge across the river, with houses on it, painted in different colours.'

'How do you know all that?'

'My father had his portrait painted, and behind him is such a city,' I said.

'My family live in a palace on the river,' said Tycho. 'Oh, Coriander, there is so much more to this world than the little fragment you have seen of it. Now that Rosmore is gone, it will be restored to the golden land it always was. I want to show you the brightly coloured houses and the merchants who trade in cloths no human eye has seen. I want to take you to the goblin market, to sail downriver in a boat pulled by mermen, so that you can listen to the songs and stories of the mermaids. I promise you with all my heart that I will love and take care of you always. Do not go. Please stay. You belong here.'

I wanted to go with him. I wanted that more than anything else, and for one moment, one wild moment, I thought I could. Then I remembered all those I had left behind. Was it not strange? Here I was. I had hoped to see Tycho again. Now my hopes tasted like bitter fruit in my mouth, and I said, 'Alas, I cannot come. I have to go back and see what has happened to my father.'

'I wish it were not so,' said Tycho. And he lifted my face towards his and kissed me. I stood there as if in a dream, unable to move.

'Then come back with me. Let me show you my city,' I said, 'and our house by the river.'

I felt happiness rush in upon me once more, only for it to recede like the tide when he said, 'I wish it could be. Like you, I have much to find out.'

I looked into his dark eyes and in them saw the planets and the stars.

'Time is the only thing that is against us,' he said, 'for our worlds are run by different clocks. Maybe I will have a long beard like Medlar when next we meet, and you will be a married woman. What then?' He kissed me again. 'Come home,' he said. 'Come back with me now.'

I felt that I stood at a crossroads between two worlds. I must choose between this land of dreams and promises, or my life, my real life in London. The decision was made all the harder by the sweetness of Tycho's touch and the longing in my heart to be with him. I was sure that whichever path I took I would never get back to this moment again, and that I would have to live with regret. I felt the silver shoes press into me, and I heard my mother's sweet voice calling, and knew then that I must return and find my father. I must for her sake put away all childish thoughts. I must for her become a young woman and accept my lot in life.

'Do you think it is enough that we met and fell in love?'

'No,' said Tycho. 'I know that with you I am complete. Without you the boy in me is for ever lost.'

'I have to return,' I said.

'I know that,' he said, and he kissed me and climbed back on to the great white horse and rode away towards the forest.

It was unbearable to see him leave and I forced myself not to look. I busied myself by taking out the silver shoes from my doublet, and carefully unwrapping them. Tears, blasted tears, blurred my vision. Only when I had the first shoe on did I allow myself to look back, to see that Tycho had stopped at the edge of the forest and was watching me. I wanted to run to him, and I felt as if my heart would break when once more he turned away and slowly rode out of sight. A part of me went with him, and as I put my foot into the other shoe I wondered if I would ever feel whole again.

*A*nd so the sixth part of my tale is told, and with it a candle goes out.

PART SEVEN

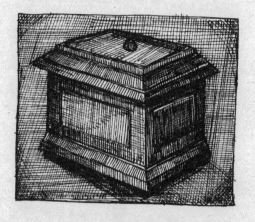

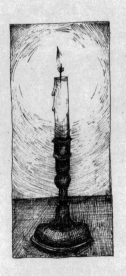

31

Homecoming

So the wheel had come full circle and I found myself back in my father's study. Mysteriously, the furniture had been restored to its rightful place. The stuffed alligator was once again king of the ebony cabinet and my mother's chest was placed under the latticed window. How strange to see it so! I wondered if Rosmore's death had had anything to do with this transformation.

I looked around the room, feeling as if I stood outside time, uncertain as to whether the hands on the clock had gone backwards or forwards. A fire was burning, and I thought the year must still be young if there was need of kindling and coal.

I heard footsteps outside the study door and quickly hid beside the ebony cabinet, wondering who would turn the handle. To my utter amazement, there was my father. He was dressed for the day's business and carrying a pile of letters, one of which he was reading. He looked older than I remembered, his hair grey and his face weather-worn.

'Father!' I whispered and he spun round, as shocked to see

me as I was to see him. His papers shot from his hands and went flying up into the air. We stood like strangers, staring at one another. I heard the clock in the hall strike the hour and in that moment I knew I had rejoined this world.

He said softly, as one might to a ghost, 'Coriander?' Puzzled, he looked at me as if still unsure whether he could trust what he was seeing. 'Am I dreaming or is it truly you, dressed so strangely?'

'It is truly I,' I replied. 'I have come back.'

Carefully, with measured steps, he came towards me and wrapped me in his arms. Only at this proof that I was flesh and blood did he to start to weep.

'I thought I had lost you,' he cried, 'I thought I had lost you.'

There was a knock on the study door. My father turned quickly, fumbling for a handkerchief, and blew his nose.

'Who is it?'

'Danes, sir.'

My father went to the door. Shielding me with his body, he opened it just wide enough to let her in and then quickly closed it.

'What is going on, sir? Are you all right? Why, what happened to your letters?'

He moved away and pointed to where I was standing.

'Oh, my goodness!' cried Danes, rushing towards me. 'Did I not tell you, sir, that she would come back to us? Oh, my little sparrow, I knew you would not fly away for good. But why are you still dressed as a boy?'

'There is no time to explain. We must get her out of those clothes,' said my father urgently.

It was too late. There came another knock on the door.

My father rushed to stop whoever it was from entering, but it was no good. There stood Mistress Bedwell with a small girl who was holding a basket.

'I came to say goodbye,' said Mistress Bedwell.

'Patience,' said my father, trying to stop her from coming any further into the room. 'You saw the baby?'

'That I did and such a healthy little fellow. He looks so like his –' She stopped, seeing the papers scattered on the floor. 'Are you all right?' she asked with concern. 'You look a little red around the eyes. Not bad news, I hope.'

'No, no, everything is fine, thank you. Let me see you to the garden gate.'

'Who is that boy? Why is he hiding?' said the child, pointing at me.

Mistress Bedwell looked over at me and her mouth fell open with surprise.

'You remember Coriander,' said my father.

'I certainly do,' she said, perplexed. 'It is wonderful to see you.' She stopped, taking in my appearance. 'But why, pray, are you dressed so?'

My father cut in quickly, 'Coriander has just returned from the country. It was thought safer for her to dress this way for her journey on account of the dangers on the road.'

'Oh, dear Lord, yes,' said Danes. 'Why, I have heard the

most terrible stories of vagabonds and highwaymen and worse. One cannot be too careful in these desperate and lawless times.'

'That of course is true. And what news of your cousin?' asked Mistress Bedwell.

I tried to look as if I knew what she was talking about.

'A miraculous recovery!' said Danes.

'Yes,' replied my father, 'by the grace of the Good Lord, he rose up from his deathbed to live another day.'

Mistress Bedwell looked even more perplexed as my father and Danes made up a story between them that was as long as it was round in the telling. It was like watching two fish floundering on the shore, trying to make a river from a puddle.

Patience Bedwell's eyes were as wide as saucers.

'What a tale! You quite take my breath away,' she said. 'At all events, Coriander, it is lovely to see you. Dear Edmund often asks after you. He will be delighted at the news of your return. Tell me,' she continued, 'what do you think of the baby?'

Again I was at a loss as to what to say. For the life of me I could not think whose baby she was talking about. 'Enchanting,' I said, hoping that was the right reply. Babies were usually thought to be so.

'Now, Master Hobie, you must bring Coriander to dine with us, though not, perhaps,' she laughed, 'in those clothes. Shall we say Wednesday? There is so much to catch up on. Edmund will be impatient to meet you and hear all about your travels.'

'By all means, with pleasure,' said my father.

'Come, Sarah,' said Mistress Bedwell to the child who still stood there, her mouth wide open, staring at me.

'Where did you get those silver shoes?' she asked.

I said they were made specially for me.

'Come,' said Danes impatiently, 'let me show you out,' and with all speed she hurried the two of them from the room.

My father closed the door firmly behind them and leaning against it said, 'I think she believed us!'

And we both burst out laughing.

'The baby,' I said. 'Father, tell me who has had a baby.'

'First,' said my father, 'you tell me how you came by your silver shoes.'

32

The Sweetest
Little Fingers

I opened the door to Hester's room and was greeted by such a lovely sight. Hester, looking beautiful, with red rosy cheeks, was sitting in a low chair. The baby, his tiny hand lying flat against her breast, sucked merrily away, making slurping noises like a bird.

Hester took her eyes lazily off the baby and said, 'Oh, sweet Coriander, I knew you would come back. I told your father so many times that you would.'

'Hester, look at you! Motherhood much becomes you,' I said.

Hester smiled. 'I am as round and as plump as a loaf of bread. I am no longer skin and bone.'

The baby stopped feeding and carefully, as if he were a flower, she handed him to me to hold.

'What is his name?' I asked.

'Joseph Appleby. We named him after my father.'

What a wonder a baby is. Such newness just waiting to unfold. Little Joseph's tiny hand was perfect in every way, his face full of dreams. He smelt of milk as he nestled into me and then, finding his fist, he sucked greedily on his fingers until he fell asleep in my arms.

'Why, look at you dressed so!' said Hester. 'You have on the same clothes you wore that fearful night when Tarbett Purman was killed.'

'I know. Although I have only been gone such a short time, so much has happened.'

'Coriander, are you dreaming? You have been gone more than a year and a half.'

'A year! It cannot be so. What then is the date?'

'I can tell you exactly, for I have counted every day since you left. This is the second day of April, and the year is 1660.'

'Tell me,' I said, 'how is it you are safely home?'

'Why,' said Hester, 'friends of the King made sure that all the charges were dropped against Gabriel. Your father saw to it.'

'Wait,' I said, 'wait! Not so fast. The King?'

'Yes, King Charles II. Has your father not told you that he has been all this time with the King in exile? He put his only remaining ship at the service of His Majesty. You should hear Sam talk of the adventures they have had.'

'Hester, you are not making any sense. What, Oliver Cromwell now takes counsel from the King? I doubt it much!'

'No, bless you! Old Noll is dead.'

'Dead?' I said.

'That is why we are home again. Now, tell me what has been happening to you,' said Hester.

'No,' I said. 'That can wait. I want to understand how you came to meet up with my father.'

'Well, it was like this. When we landed at La Rochelle, we were at a loss as to what to do. We were in immediate need of work and coin but we did not know whom we could trust. There were many English refugees in the town and all sorts of alarming rumours which in the event amounted to nothing at all. Just as our money was running out, whom did we spy?' She stopped and looked at the baby and touched his hands. 'Are they not the sweetest little fingers you ever did see, so small and delicate?'

'Yes, yes, Hester. They are the most beautiful fingers a baby could have. Now tell me for the love of the Lord, whom did you spy?'

'Why, Sam, your father's apprentice.'

'What was he doing there?' I asked.

'That was the luck of it. Your father's ship was in port and he had come to meet it. He told us that your father was fair desperate for news of you.' Again Hester stopped and said, 'Is not the baby the spitting image of Gabriel?'

'Hester, please,' I begged, 'tell me what happened without all the stopping and starting, for you are making me giddy in the telling.'

'Forgive me,' said Hester. 'I do not know what it is about having a baby, but I can hardly put my mind to think on anything else.'

'For my sake, try,' I pleaded.

'I told your father all about my mother and Arise Fell. I left out nothing. I said how you had come to be locked in the chest and how, against all the wonders of the world, you came out again, though you had been gone for all of three summers. Then Gabriel told him about the night when Tarbett Purman died and how he had come to be accused of murder.

'Well, when your father set sail again he took us with him. When it was safe to return to England, he insisted that we both live in Thames Street. I showed him the papers you had gone to the trouble of writing for me. He took Gabriel into his employment and I asked if he would let me work for him too. Do you know what he said?'

I shook my head.

'He said that no daughter of his would ever work as a maid. He would not hear of it. Can you believe that? After all I had told him, he called me his daughter! He said that he would never think of me in any other light.'

And she started to cry.

'Oh Hester, dry your eyes. You will make the baby cry.'

'Do you think it was wrong of him?'

'I would have expected no less. You are my sister, dear Hester, no matter what.'

'How could anyone harm a baby?' said Hester.

'I do not know,' I said, looking at Joseph's mop of dark hair. 'My mother did.'

'Hester, you are not she.'

'I know, but it saddens me to think of it. I cannot for the life of me understand it. Are you tired? You can put him in the cradle if you wish, Coriander.'

'No, I like having him in my arms.'

She laughed. 'So do I. I like him to sleep close to me. Danes say it is better than leaving him alone in a cradle to get too cold or too hot. Mistress Bedwell does not agree. She says that I should have a wet nurse and not hold him all the time, for it indulges him so.'

I laughed. 'What nonsense!'

Hester looked pleased. 'It feels right, him being next to me.'

'Hester, do what you feel is best. Take no notice of Patience Bedwell.'

I could hear the sound of boots on the stairs.

'Coriander!' said Gabriel, coming into the room. He looked as proud as ever I saw him and quite the man. 'It is so good to see you. I could hardly believe the news when Danes told me that you had returned.'

I got up and he took little Joseph from me.

'Have I not a fine son?' he said, going to sit beside his wife.

'I have been trying to find out from Hester how long it is since you have been back,' I said.

'Just four months, since this January. We heard that the country had no more appetite for being a republic and the talk was all of the King's return. Your father was full of grief not to find you here when we finally came home.'

'I kept telling him that you would be all right,' said Hester, 'that you had come back before and you would again.'

'It has been awkward, though,' said Gabriel, 'for neighbours and friends seemed to have more questions in them than we could find answers for.'

'You should see Bridge Street,' said Hester, changing the subject. 'Should she not, Gabriel? It has all been repainted, flags are being put up and nearly every shop has *By Appointment to the King* hanging from its sign. It looks so pretty, Coriander.'

Gabriel put his arm round Hester. 'That it does,' he said, and he looked on his little family with pride.

I left them and went back downstairs to find my father waiting for me in the hall below.

'I still cannot believe you have come home,' he said.

33

To the King his Own

That evening, after I had bathed and dressed in clean clothes, I sat with my father in his study, enjoying the heat from the fire. We were, I thought, like two travellers returned from faraway places to tell of our different journeys, only to find that our maps had overlapped.

'Do you forgive me?' he asked.

'For what?'

'For leaving you with Maud and that preacher.'

'You were not to know what they would do.'

'No,' he said, getting up to poke the fire and sending sparks like dragons' breath up the chimney. 'But I should not have been so wrapped up in my own grief. I should have taken better care of you and of our future.'

'You did your best.'

'In truth I was tortured by the thought of your mother's shadow. I kept the casket in here for safety's sake . . .'

'I know. I saw it. One evening when I could not sleep, I came down the stairs into the study to find you at your desk with the casket. The lid was open and you asked me if you should have given it back to her.'

'Did I?' he said, looking at me. 'I do not remember. I was too consumed by my own misery.'

'Father,' I said, trying to reassure him, 'you were brave enough to do what she wished for.'

'Brave, you call it. No, not brave, foolhardy,' he said. 'She gave me her shadow on our wedding night. She made me promise that I would always keep it safe. I did not understand what she meant. I tried to give it back to her when she was ill. She would have none of it. I should have taken it out of the casket and forced it on her. Oh, what a fool I was!' And he hit the wall above the fireplace with his hand.

'You did what she wanted,' I said.

'Yes, and she died. If I had made her take the shadow, would she still be alive?'

'She would have been alive for a while in her world, and then she would have been killed by her stepmother, Queen Rosmore, who was waiting to take the shadow from her. Father, believe me, you did the right thing. It was Rosmore who killed her. That is why none of the remedies worked. But she wanted to die in this world with us. She did not want to go back where she had come from.'

My father came to sit beside me and held my hand.

'She knew that if that happened, you and she would be parted for ever,' I went on. 'She took her chance with death in this world, hoping that by the grace of the Lord you would one day be reunited. That could never have happened if you had given her back her shadow.'

'Coriander, how do you know these things? If what you say is true you have taken a great weight off my shoulders.'

'It is true, Father. I promise you that it is.'

He looked back at the fire and after a while said, 'What has happened to the shadow?'

'It is mine to look after now, and it is where it should be.'

'And the silver shoes,' my father went on. 'I could not understand why Eleanor was so adamant that you should not have them. When she told me that she thought her stepmother had put a spell on them, it made no sense. In all honesty I felt it was easier not to believe it.'

'What did she tell you?' I asked.

'That those silver shoes had been sent to you to tempt you into her world. She told me about her stepmother and how she was sure that she would try to find the shadow, and that if she did, then one day we would lose you.'

'Why did she think that?' I asked.

'Because you come from her world as much as ours.'

'Surely you must have been in that land too,' I said, 'for I have seen a portrait of you with mermaids by a river.'

'Those paintings were sent to us after our wedding. Eleanor told me that they were a present from her father. I never met him; I never went to that land. I often wondered how it was they had got such a good likeness of me. Oh Coriander, I should never have left you. I should have taken you with me, as you asked me to do. I have never forgotten your sweet face looking up at mine and your thin little arms around my neck. If only I could turn back time! Instead, like a fool, I left, telling myself it was all for the best.'

'Maybe it was,' I said.

Danes came in with a tankard of ale and a plate of seed cake. She set them down on the table and said, 'Have you told her about Maud?'

'No,' I said. 'Please do. What happened to her?'

My father let out a hollow laugh. 'She was found babbling here in the house,' he said, 'by a pile of bones which she swore were the remains of Arise Fell. The constable had her arrested and as they could make neither head nor tail of what she was saying, she was taken to Newgate Jail. She was accused of murder.'

'They were the bones of Arise Fell,' I said.

'If that is the case, I am glad to know it. There was much talk of the preacher, for he was not seen again. When I got back to London, I came straight here. I could hardly believe the state or the stench of the house, all the furniture gone, and rats the only inhabitants. I was so angry I went to see Maud in prison. She was not a pretty sight, given over to boils and sores on the skin. Lord, I felt so angry with her that I wanted her hanged. She begged and wept, saying that she had lost her way, that it was all the work of the Devil. I would have none of it. That brought her up sober and no mistake. She told me that she and Arise had been given gold by some old witch. All they had to do was kill you and find the shadow for her, but evidently they tried to play the woman for a fool, which they much regretted. Maud spoke all the time in the plural, as if Arise was still by her side.'

'What happened to Maud? Was she hanged?'

'She pleaded with me to get her freed and promised that if I did she would reveal where all my furniture could be found.'

'Was it at Ludgate Meeting House?' I asked, smiling.

'Yes,' said my father. 'The wretched brethren had all my things. Arise and Maud had removed everything with the exception of the stuffed alligator. I made a statement to the authorities and Maud and the entire congregation were deported to the New World.'

'I think,' said Danes quietly, 'that she had much to thank you for.'

'I could not, for Hester's sake, see her mother hanged. The poor girl had had more than her share of troubles. I only regret that Danes was not able to find me when she came to France.'

'I regret too, sir, that our paths never crossed,' said Danes. 'I feared that you were dead.'

As May came into blossom, Charles II was proclaimed King of England. All London became giddy with the thought, like a tipsy old widow putting on her finery after years of mourning. Everyone's spirits suddenly lifted. The hope for the future was good and the cry on every street corner was 'To the King his own!'

On the day after my return, Danes took me to see Master Thankless. Hester was right: Bridge Street was hardly recognisable. It was undergoing a feverish transformation. Buildings were being painted, windows mended, flags hung out for the King, who was due to enter London over the great bridge. A maypole with the King's flag on it had been put up near Bridge Street, and although some soldiers tried to have it removed it stayed firmly upright.

The streets were awash with colour. Never in this world had I seen such a collection of brightly dressed people as there were on Thames Street that morning. Gone were the sober blacks and greys. Now defiant scarlet, pink, yellow and purple met the eye.

It was official. The country had sent the Puritans packing and it was hard to believe that anyone had ever supported Oliver Cromwell.

On our way we bumped into Mistress Jones, who was full of complaints about the money being spent and the fuss being made.

'If we cannot celebrate the King's return, what can we celebrate?' said Danes.

'Hmm,' said Mistress Jones. 'I think we shall all live to regret the day we asked him to come back. In my view, we should have kept to being a God-fearing Republic.'

Danes drew herself up. 'How can you say that? Oliver Cromwell was nothing but a usurper.'

'Come,' I said hastily, taking her arm, 'we shall never get all our errands done if we stand here all day arguing.'

'Why, some people . . .' she said as we neared the tailor's shop.

I had to smile. 'At least Mistress Jones is making no disguise of the fact that she supported Oliver Cromwell. I suspect that if we asked these other folk, we would find it hard to get a single one of them to confess to being a Puritan.'

The bell to the shop rang out merrily and Nell opened the door. Her hand flew to her face when she saw me.

'Oh, take me to sea in a sieve! You're back safe!' she said. 'And what a fine lady you are, to be sure! You'd turn the King's head.'

Master Thankless looked up from his cutting table.

'Coriander!' he said, coming over and kissing me on the cheek. 'I told you, Mary, she would come back looking more beautiful than ever.'

'Is all going well?' I asked.

'I feel like a lord,' said the tailor. 'And if business keeps on like this, I shall be richer than the King. Why, everyone wants new clothes. They want to look as bright as peacocks' tails, as colourful as parakeets.'

He took us down to the kitchen and opened a bottle of Rhenish wine. The fresh-faced new apprentice, Tom, brought in bolts of fabric for us to look at.

'I have been told that you are in need of new gowns in the latest French fashions,' said Master Thankless.

'That is right,' I said, feeling very merry, for it is a pleasant and cheerful thing to have a new gown made.

Master Thankless went to no end of trouble to show me all his fine fabrics, winking as he said he kept these only for his favourite customers. In the end I settled upon a flowered satin gown of pale green and to go with it a petticoat of striped silk. Then I chose a bodice made of water-marked taffeta with full sleeves, trimmed with silver lace and pearls, and to top it all, a cut skirt to be tied back so that my pretty petticoats could be seen.

'Well,' said Master Thankless when all the measuring and the patterns had been agreed, 'by my word, you will look a princess. Now, has Danes told you the news?'

'No,' I said uncertain as to what news he meant. Danes blushed, which was most unlike her, and said, 'Of course I have not. We agreed to wait until we were all together again.'

'What is this news?' I asked.

Master Thankless held Danes's hand and said with a smile as big as his face, 'Mistress Danes – Mary – has consented to marry me.'

'No!' I said, jumping up. 'Why, that is wonderful! I am so pleased for you!' And I kissed them both soundly.

'Who would ever have thought it?' said Danes, flustered. 'I truly believed I was too old to be loved.'

'Never,' teased Master Thankless. 'Age has only added to your charms.'

34
The Perfect Wife

Although surrounded by so much happiness, I often felt sad. I would look at my father and at Danes, at Hester and her baby, and suddenly, like a beam of sunlight in a shuttered room, I would be transported in my mind to that other world, to Tycho and all that I had had to leave behind.

I knew that in returning, I had made the right decision. This is what my mother wished for me, here my future lay, but this knowledge did not still my sense of regret.

I was not helped by the Bedwells, who had come to the conclusion that I would make Edmund the perfect wife. In fact, this seemed to be taken as a matter of course by everyone except me. Apparently, there was no greater asset to a father than an unmarried daughter, as long as that unmarried daughter did not take too long in finding herself a suitable husband.

'I am not agreeing to marry a man I have not seen since I was a child,' I said to my father. I was sitting in my chamber and Danes was dressing my hair and placing in it some flowers.

'Of course not, my poppet,' he said, 'though I am sure you

will be most impressed with Edmund. I have heard that he is a very clever, personable young man with a bright future. He wants to get into Parliament.'

What could I say? That I was not a parcel to be bought or shipped? Danes pulled the laces of my dress tight as my father continued.

'He is an ambitious young man and my happiness would be complete to see not only the King restored but my daughter settled.'

'I have only just come back, and already you want me gone,' I said.

My father's face fell.

'No, that is not what I am saying. I only want what is best for you. I do not want to lose you ever again.'

Oh, how I wanted to tell him about Tycho. I looked quickly at Danes but I could tell by her expression that she thought I should keep him to myself.

On Wednesday, as promised, we were invited to luncheon at the Bedwells', and Danes helped me dress in my new gown. I have never been one for staring vainly at myself in the looking glass, but even I was somewhat surprised and gladdened by what I saw. I was a fine young lady. Danes stood there saying I near shamed the sun itself. My father agreed, saying he had never seen me look more lovely. He was wearing his new periwig with many a fine curl hanging down, good wide lace at the neck, and a suit of plum velvet with an embroidered coat. We looked a grand pair indeed, said Danes, and even though the

Bedwells' house was no distance, my father sent for a sedan chair to take us there.

The luncheon was a formal one where we spoke only of things that mattered not a jot to anyone present, the conversation being as shallow as a silver serving dish.

I had, in all truth, been curious to see Edmund again. We were placed next to each other and he took my hand and kissed it extravagantly, all the while looking round at the other guests. I knew immediately that he was not for me. He was as full of his own virtues as some women are full of their modesty. For the whole meal, he talked about what he had achieved since he had left Cambridge. You could be forgiven for thinking that he alone had brought about the King's restoration. In short, the man was a good-looking, boring, conceited fool.

After luncheon was over, we went upriver on the Bedwells' barge.

'A perfect match; they are made for one another,' I overheard Mistress Bedwell whisper to my father.

I sat with Edmund, feeling stiff and awkward and sure that Danes had tied my laces too tight. I had very few words, which mattered not to Edmund for as long as he could hear his own voice he seemed more than content. I took in the view of all the little boats that looked so pretty, and felt in the air the excitement of a city on the brink of change. The riverbanks were turning green again and houses that had been neglected had been newly painted. The taverns were full and as we passed, we could hear shouts for the King ring out, skimming the water like pebbles.

'The theatres are to be opened again. The King is all for the play,' said Edmund. 'We should make an outing of it.'

There was no need for me to reply. I just had to smile and look interested, in short be nothing more than a doll, a pleasing poppet.

We went as far as Whitehall, which was being made ready for the King's return, and saw the stone gallery which is mighty long, and I thought that this was where the King's father must have walked on his way to his execution. Oh, how the tide had turned!

The palace was bustling with people and Edmund seemed more than a little annoyed to see that the riff-raff, as he called them, were allowed in. One young man took off his plumed hat and bowed at me in an elaborate manner.

'What a silken fop,' said Edmund, pointing at the young man. 'He has so much ribbon about him, he looks as if he has plundered six shops and set up twenty country pedlars.'

Mistress Bedwell said Edmund was a most amusing young fellow, which I did not think boded well for her sense of humour.

We walked through the Privy Garden before going back to the Bedwells' house, where we said our farewells. I had enjoyed being out on the river again and seeing Whitehall, and watching so many people go by. It brought colour to my cheeks, which Edmund took to be a sign that I was much taken with him. No doubt he thought our marriage was a foregone conclusion.

'Coriander,' called Hester when we returned. 'Come quick! I have such wondrous news to tell you.' I went upstairs to her chamber to find Joseph fast asleep in his cradle and Hester sitting on the edge of the bed.

'Hester, what are you doing? Should you not be resting?' I said.

'I have been resting, but you will never guess who is here,' she said excitedly.

'Who?'

'My brother Ned. He has just arrived. He has been all over the country trying to find me. Can you believe it?'

There was a knock on the door and there was Danes with a freshly laundered gown.

'Coriander, your father wants you to come down and meet the visitor,' said Danes. I smoothed out my skint and ran down to the study.

Ned Jarret was a big man, red-faced and with red hands. He had such a look of Maud about him that to begin with I felt anxious. It was only when he talked that all similarities with Maud ended, for a kinder, sweeter man would have been hard to find, and his story was a sorrowful one and most touching.

It appeared that he had got caught up in the fighting and joined Cromwell's New Model Army. It was not until years later that he came across his father, living in penury in Birmingham.

Ned had been bruised about the head. He was much haunted by the dark things he had seen, and had little appetite for living. He took care of his father as best he could and later they were glad to find work in the North Country with a farmer who had lost all his sons in the fighting and needed help on the land, even from broken men. The two of them lived together in peace.

This much he told us before Hester came down. My father and I left them to talk, for it was clear that Hester wanted to be alone with her brother.

We were a large group to sit down that night for supper: Danes, Master Thankless, Hester and Gabriel, Sam, Ned, my father and me. The candles were guttering before half the stories were told.

'Tell me, Ned,' said Gabriel, 'how long has it taken you to find Hester?'

Ned said very quietly, 'I wish I had had a mind to look for her earlier, but my head was so muddled with memories of bloodshed that I could not think straight. When at last I went back to our village I was told all manner of tales, and I truly did not know who or what to believe.'

'Is your father still alive?' asked my father.

'No, sir, he has been dead since last Michaelmas, God rest his soul.'

'I am sorry to hear it, and I am sorry too that you did not find Hester sooner.'

'So am I, for I would dearly love to have seen my father again and to have looked after you both,' said Hester with tears in her eyes.

Ned took hold of her hand. 'You were always in our prayers.'

Hester sobbed, and after a while my father said, 'I must tell you, my dear sir, that you have released me from a tide of woes. To know that my marriage to Maud Leggs is more than dubious is a joy indeed.'

'You cannot be married to her, sir. Surely there is no law that allows a woman to have two husbands at one time.'

'Ned,' said my father, 'I assure you that I married your mother believing her to be a widow woman whose husband was killed in the war.'

'I can credit that,' said Ned. 'She was a fearsome woman with little goodness or softness about her. When I was small, I thought she was the storm made real. She had had a hard life, one that had made her all the harder.'

Hester rested her head on her brother's shoulder.

'I was at my wits' end to think I might never see you again. I did not care what befell our mother,' said Ned, 'but I loved you dearly, Hester. You were such a brave little girl and so sorely used. I lay awake many nights wondering about your fate. I expected to find you in a bad way from all the talk I had heard about my mother and the preacher. I am overjoyed to find you married and well settled in life.'

That night was the merriest I could remember for a long time. I thought what an odd collection we were, a Roundhead who had fought for Cromwell and Royalists who had supported the King, each one willing to die for his beliefs, and yet here we all were with more to unite us than divide us.

'This country has been torn apart,' said Ned. 'Brother against brother, father against son. Nothing good can come about when a dog starts to eat his own tail.'

'Hear, hear,' said my father. 'This is a new decade and a new beginning. Let us hope this king will find a way to heal the wounds. Let the fountains run with wine, not blood.'

Hester said quietly, 'Master Hobie, if my mother was never married to you . . .'

'The best thing that came with your mother was you,' said my father. 'Why, look what a family I have. Now, that is something to be proud of.'

'I quite agree,' I said, 'for I would never have had a brave and lovely sister had Maud not come into our lives.'

*E*ver since the luncheon with the Bedwells, Edmund had called each day to see me, whether he was welcome or not. In truth I began to dread his visits. I wished I could feel something for him, but I did not.

'He is a good-looking man,' said Hester.

'I am sure he is,' I replied.

'He is clever. Why, Gabriel said he could talk Wednesday into Sunday if he had a mind to.'

'I do not doubt it. Oh Hester, I feel nothing for him, nothing.'

'You well might in time. Why, many a man and woman

who marry in this fair city do not think much of each other at first, and later fall in love.'

'Hester, would you have married Gabriel and run away with him if you did not love him?'

'No,' said Hester. 'But that is different. I mean –'

'No it is not,' I interrupted. 'I would rather not marry at all than marry a man I cared naught for.'

'Oh dear,' said Hester. 'You have it bad for someone. That much I can see.'

All I could do was nod, for sobs were doing their best to make a fool of me.

The more Edmund pushed himself upon me, the more I missed Tycho. Why could I not be left in peace, given a chance to recover myself? Then maybe I would feel differently for Edmund, though I doubted it.

At night, alone in my chamber, I would look at my silver shoes and long for a different ending to my story. I could not sleep, I did not care to eat: in short, everything in me felt unsettled and jangled about. I almost regretted my decision to come back. I would have to dry my eyes and tell myself not to be childish.

No doubt my behaviour led everyone to believe that I was in love with Edmund, who clearly thought that it was his God-given right to have me as his wife. Quite how this all had come about so quickly, and without my compliance, baffled me and made me feel guilty too. In truth, I felt nothing for Edmund Bedwell and I longed for him to disappear. All I could think was that in life people prefer things to be tidy and I suppose a marriage is, after all, a familiar knot.

It was coming up to the end of May. Our household, like the rest of London, was preoccupied with the return of the King. Everyone wanted the day to go well and each family made their own plans for the celebration. Those fortunate enough to have houses that overlooked the route he was to take suddenly found they had many new friends.

The tailor's shop had without doubt one of the best views. The plan was to go to Master Thankless early in the day, before the streets became too crowded. The whole of London was expected to turn out.

There was much excitement in our household because my father had been asked to accompany the King on his ride back to Whitehall. There was talk that he would be given a knight-hood for services rendered to His Majesty. When Danes heard the news, she looked as if she was floating on air, so proud was she of my father. 'Oh sir,' she said, wiping her eyes, 'Eleanor always told me that you would be a great man one day.'

The evening before, Edmund had come to our house and said that he wanted to talk to my father alone. I watched him from the landing. England was free of its tyrant and yet with every turn of the hourglass I felt my freedom slip away like the sands of time.

Edmund left without asking to see me and I felt much relief when the door closed behind him. Then my father called me to his study. He was dressed in travelling clothes, his saddlebag waiting by the front door, in readiness to join the King's party and ride behind the King on his triumphant journey through the City.

'Do you know what Edmund wanted?' he asked.

I felt sick and leaden in the pit of my stomach. I knew what he was going to say.

'Edmund has asked for your hand in marriage. He put it most excellently,' said my father. 'He gave all manner of good reasons why you should be his wife. Your admirer has it all planned out.'

'I wish much that he would leave me in peace,' I said peevishly.

'Well, he seems to have his mind set upon marrying you, and you could do a good deal worse.'

'But Father, I do not love him. I never will.' Then I said something that took even me by surprise. 'I love someone else.'

There, I had spoken the words.

My father stood looking out of the window at the river. The bells had started to ring out.

'I feared this,' he said, turning back to look at me. 'It is written all over you. Who is this person? Where is he?'

'He comes from my mother's world. He is a prince. His name is Tycho. I left him to come home to you. There is no need to worry. I will never see him again,' I said sadly.

'When I met your mother that day on the road by the oak tree,' said my father, 'I fell in love with her at once. I would have followed her to the ends of the earth. The greatest fortune in my life was that she felt the same way. I cannot force you to marry a man you do not care for. What folly that would be. You must be true to your heart, Coriander.'

'That is the trouble, Father. My heart is not here, not in this world, and I am torn apart,' I said.

'My poor Coriander,' said my father. 'I must confess I thought that if you were to marry Edmund, you would stay. In truth I could not bear losing you again. I know one thing. If your mother were alive, she would tell you to be brave and true to what you feel. It is what she did. I can see that Edmund would never make you happy, and to rub along together is, I can assure you, not enough. I ask only that you wait until the King has returned. If then you decide to put on your silver shoes, I will understand.'

'Father, it is too late,' I said.

'I hope not.' And he kissed me and left the room and I stood in the study looking at the Thames flowing past, and cried, pulled like the river's current between two worlds.

35

A Fool and his Periwig

*L*ondon awoke to a chorus of bells that have so long been silent, chiming once again for the coming of the King. The very air seems charged with excitement.

Early in the morning Edmund came round to ask me to marry him. He chose the worst moment, when the house was in turmoil. There he stood, in the middle of the hall, dressed in a new suit with a coat that went down to his knees and silk stockings up to his breeches and bows on his shoes. He was wearing a grand periwig that fitted him ill, making his face look small and mean.

'Coriander, pray, I would like a word in private,' he said as Hester rushed down the stairs with the baby, who just that moment had been sick on his new gown. In the kitchen I heard a pan drop and clatter loudly on the stone floor. Ned pushed past us in his shirtsleeves with a bowl of water.

'We will never be ready in time,' I heard Danes say.

Edmund took no notice and opened the door to the study as if it was already his own.

'Please, can it wait?' I pleaded. 'This is not a good time.'

'On such an auspicious day? I can think of none better,' he said, moving me firmly into the study and closing the door on all the familiar, friendly noises of the house.

'I want you to be my wife.'

I could not think what to say except a blunt no. My lack of response in no way silenced Edmund.

'Ours would be, as I am sure you will agree, a most perfect match. Both our families have much to gain from our marriage. I have already spoken to your father. Naturally, in return for my good name, I would expect you to run a neat and tidy home, bring the children up in a God-fearing manner and at all times obey,' and here he smiled a thin smile, 'indeed, worship me as your husband.'

I felt like bursting out laughing and had to bite the inside of my mouth to keep myself from doing so, but Edmund, unaware, carried on just as if I had agreed to his proposal.

'As you know, I am set on entering Parliament and I would require my wife to stand beside me in all matters.' He turned so that I could see his sharp, unforgiving features and took out a pressed handkerchief into which he blew his nose loudly.

Oh please hurry up and be gone, I thought, hoping that someone would come to look for me and so distract him.

He cleared his throat. 'Coriander, I have consulted some prominent friends and we agree that it may be best for you to be known simply as Ann Bedwell. It is a more fitting name for a Member of Parliament's wife.'

I replied as kindly as I could that I thought he must have asked the wrong people, for my name was Coriander and there was no question of changing it.

'I just meant . . .' he said, somewhat flustered by my answer.

'I know perfectly well what you mean,' I said. 'You wish me to look like myself and yet be someone else. I cannot do it. I have had my name taken from me once before. I had to fight to get it back. My name is Coriander. I am not the Ann you are looking for.'

'I suggest,' said Edmund, 'that you reflect on my offer before making a hasty decision which you may come to regret.'

'My answer, sir, is no.'

Danes saved me. She bustled into the study, unaware of Edmund's presence.

'We really must be going, my sparrow. The barge is waiting to take us to the bridge. We do not want to miss a moment of this wonderful day.'

'Really, madam,' said Edmund sharply, 'should you not knock before you come in? This is not a barn.'

Danes looked surprised to be spoken to in such a manner. I thought she was about to give him a piece of her mind when Gabriel came in.

'Come on, sweet mistresses. Everyone is waiting for you. Do you need a ride, sir?' he said, on seeing Edmund.

'Pray, is there no privacy in this house?' said Edmund, ignoring him.

I took Danes's arm and left the room, feeling like a canary

newly released from its cage. We went down the steps to the water gate where everyone, including Hester with baby Joseph, was waiting in the barge.

I could not help remembering the day that Gabriel and I had come here to face Maud and Arise. Gabriel looked at me as if we were both thinking the same thing, and he smiled at me and squeezed my hand.

As we came out of the gates into bright sunshine the Thames had never looked more festive. Every boat, barge and ferry was bedecked with ribbons and flowers. People were singing and waving as if the whole of London was acquainted and I felt a surge of excitement. I knew that something extraordinary was about to happen.

We landed at the steps beside the bridge and joined the throng of people, all trying to get the best position to see the royal procession. We pushed our way through the crowds until we reached Master Thankless's shop. Nell was waiting for us.

'I am so pleased to see you,' she said. 'You would not believe how many people have offered good coin to join our party, for we will have such a fine view from here.'

'I hope you turned them all away,' said Danes, concerned.

'Of course I did,' laughed Nell, standing by the shop door like a guard dog. 'Just look at the street, the way it is strewn with flowers! Can you believe that we are really going to see His Majesty? I think I may faint when he passes.'

The shop looked quite different. All the bolts of cloth had been cleared away and on the counter roast ham, beef, chicken, pies, sweetmeats, oranges and the first strawberries of the season had been laid out.

'What do you think of that?' said Nell proudly.

'I think,' said Gabriel, 'that it looks like for a feast fit for a king.'

Master Thankless came to greet us with glasses of champagne. We were a very merry party and from the upstairs window the view down Bridge Street could not have been better. We could see everything. Down below, the crowds were packed tight. People were climbing out of windows and sitting on rooftops so that they might catch a glimpse of the royal procession. The bridge itself was hung with cloths of gold and windows were draped with silver tapestries. Everything shone in the morning sunlight.

'When Oliver Cromwell entered the City, no one threw flowers in his path,' said Danes, taking care not to call him Old Noll for fear of upsetting Ned.

'I remember it well,' said Master Thankless. 'We were fair terrified in case the army took a fancy to killing any Londoners they met on their way. Now look how the tide has turned.'

We had to wait a long while to see the King, but when he reached Traitors' Gate we heard a great shout go up from the crowd, so that even before we saw him we knew he was coming.

What can I tell you about the moment the King appeared? We leant out of the window to wave and cheer. I thought he looked magical, all dressed in white and gold, with his long dark hair and handsome face, smiling as he turned this way and that to acknowledge his subjects. Hester held up the baby, Danes wept and Nell had to be held back for fear of falling out of the window, so keen was she to touch the King. Such was the emotion that even Ned, a Puritan to his very toes, looked pleased.

Suddenly I felt a strange sensation. Everything went out of focus. All I could see was the King on his great white charger. I gazed at the horse as if transfixed. His mane and coat shone bright, as if lit up from within by moonshine, and as I watched he shook his head and stared straight into my eyes. My heart raced. Could it be so? Was such a thing possible? I hardly dared whisper the thought to myself.

Then, just as swiftly, all was as it had been before: the bells, the noise, the cheering, the procession, the King and his horse passing by.

'Are you all right, Coriander?' said Danes. 'You look as if you have seen a ghost.'

'Excuse me. I need some air,' I said.

'Come closer to the window,' said Ned, stepping aside.

'No thank you. I will go downstairs.' I left the chamber quickly. I had the clear feeling that I must get back to my house.

I opened the shop door to find Edmund standing there barring my way. He took hold of my arm and moved me back into the shop, closing the door firmly behind him.

'As you know, I have spoken to your father. My family are

with Alderman Harcourt and wish me to escort you to them so that we may make our announcement.'

'I need air,' I said as I tried to pass him.

He caught hold of me. 'I can see that my proposal came as a surprise to you.'

I looked at him, amazed. 'Sir, can you not understand that I care nothing for you? I will never marry you. Never.'

'I think you will live to regret your decision,' said Edmund coldly, holding on to my arm all the tighter.

I pulled myself free. 'Leave me alone. You are a fool, Edmund Bedwell,' I said, and I picked up my skirts and ran out into the throng of people. I could hear Edmund behind me as I twisted and turned, finally losing him. The crowds pressed on me like shoals of fishes, the noise deafening. I passed maypoles and merrymakers, all dressed in their best and all in high spirits. I was certain that I saw Medlar, his lantern bobbing along. Then he was gone, as the cry went up, 'The fountains are running with wine!' and the noise blew like the wind over and into the crowd who surged forward in response.

I ran and ran, forcing myself onward. I stopped at the garden gate, my heart thumping in my chest. I straightened out my skirt and pulled down my bodice. My hair having come undone, I reached up to pin back the heavy ringlets. 'Please let me not be wrong,' I said out loud. 'Please!' Trembling, I lifted the latch.

For a moment I thought it was nothing more than a trick of the light or a tear in my eye, for my mother's garden was alight with colour, brighter than it had ever been before. The rosemary, the thyme, the coriander, the mint, the roses, the marigolds and lavender shimmered like jewels. I ran my hand through the flowers and as I did so butterflies rose up and fluttered towards the sun, beating their wings in tune with my heart.

The garden seemed empty but then I turned and looked at the door to my house. There on the steps he stood, glimmering as if in a heat haze. Fearful that my eyes might be deceiving me, I walked slowly up the path towards him.

He came into focus. Tycho! There was Tycho.

'You came!'

He took my face in his hands.

'Coriander, how could I lose you? You are my shadow. You are my light. Will you be mine, Coriander?'

I threw my arms around him and in that moment I knew that this world and the world beneath the silvery mirror had become one, all was well and the future was ours for the taking.

*D*awn is breaking and the watchman is calling in the new day. My tale is told, written not by this world's hourglass. With this, I blow out the last candle.

293

If we shadows have offended,
Think but this and all is mended:
That you have but slumbered here,
While these visions did appear.

William Shakespeare
A Midsummer Night's Dream

Some Historical Background

This story is set in the period of the Commonwealth, after the Royalists had lost the Civil War and King Charles I had been executed at Whitehall in January 1649. It was the time of a great experiment – England's one attempt to get rid of the monarchy and become a republic – and what happened in the 1640s and 50s made Parliament and the monarchy what they are today.

It is hard for us to understand how shocked people were by the execution of the King. Up to that point it was believed that the monarch was there by divine right, chosen by God to rule over His people and to be Head of the Church of England. Charles I believed completely in the divine right of kings. He was married to a Roman Catholic Queen, which did not make him popular. He was not a good politician or a wise ruler, and he made many bad and foolish decisions that ultimately led to the start of the Civil War.

The Civil War brought bitter and bloody battles that

divided families and neighbours, spoilt the land and caused great suffering and even starvation among the people. There were two camps, Royalists, who supported the King, and Puritans (also known as Roundheads because of their cropped hair). The Puritans were strong Protestants who desired to reform the Church of England and prevent it from falling back into the arms of the Roman Catholic Church. They believed that only the Bible represented the authority of God, and that Sunday should be kept for prayer and the singing of Psalms. Activities such as dancing, acting, singing and playing music were thought frivolous. Oliver Cromwell was their great champion and general of their army, called the New Model Army.

The Civil War ended with the execution of the King. There followed ten years of the Commonwealth under the leadership of Oliver Cromwell. Cromwell closed all the playhouses and banned Christmas and Christmas pudding. Maypoles were not allowed, and anyone not attending church was fined. Many old churches were ransacked, their stained glass windows broken, and religious relics burnt, for worship was to be kept simple.

All sorts of radical Protestant sects suddenly emerged: the Levellers, the Ranters, the Quakers, the Diggers and many more, some more extreme in their beliefs than others. Among them were the Fifth Monarchists. They were fundamentalists, and believed that England had to be cleared of all its sinners. Only then would the fifth reign be established, that of Lord

Jesus Christ, who would come to take up the crown of England. For a time they held great political sway, but in the end even Oliver Cromwell found their demands too far-fetched and would no longer entertain them.

London was relatively untouched by the Civil War, mainly because the King abandoned his capital for Oxford. Then, when it looked as if Cromwell was going to win the war, it was sensibly decided not to close the gates of London Bridge but to allow him to come in unchallenged.

The late King's sons and his wife Queen Henrietta Maria had taken refuge abroad some time before, but in 1653 his eldest son, Prince Charles, came back to Scotland where he was crowned King and gathered together an army to fight Cromwell at the Battle of Worcester. Although the King fought bravely, his army was no match for Cromwell's. Defeated, and with a price on his head, nineteen-year-old Charles went on the run. He had many narrow escapes and even had to hide in an oak tree while soldiers came with dogs to sniff him out, but after six weeks he managed to escape to France.

Oliver Cromwell found that peace is harder to manage than war. He wreaked vengeance on all those who had supported the Royalist cause, confiscating lands and money. It was wise in those days to be seen as a good Puritan. Cromwell had, in fact, as much trouble with Parliament as Charles I had experienced. In the end he virtually became a dictator. He was offered the ultimate prize, the crown, but refused it, preferring to keep the title he had been given in 1653, that of Lord Protector.

Cromwell died in September 1658. His son Richard, nick-named Tumbledown Dick, took over, but he had none of his father's gifts for leadership. It was General Monck, one of Cromwell's staunchest supporters, who saw that England lurched on the brink of another civil war and took the brave decision, much against the will of the army, to invite Charles II back to be King of England. And so began the Restoration.

Also by Sally Gardner

THE RED NECKLACE
Paris, 1789.

While the aristocracy dine, dance, gossip and gamble their way to disaster, the poor and starving dream of revolution.

Enter the boy Yann Margoza, destined to be a hero; Têtu the dwarf, his friend and mentor; Sido, unloved daughter of the foolish Marquis de Villeduval; and the sinister Count Kallikovski, who holds half the aristocracy in thrall to him.

The drama moves from Paris to London and back, as the Revolution gathers momentum, and the hope of liberty and the dream of equality are crushed beneath the wheel of terror.

Too many secrets, too many murders, and the blade of the guillotine is yet to fall . . .

(available from October 2007)

By Kevin Crossley-Holland

THE SEEING STONE

Set in the Welsh Marches in the year 1199, *The Seeing Stone* is a unique take on the Arthurian legends.

In a hundred short chapters that seem like snapshots of the past, *The Seeing Stone* brilliantly evokes the earthy, uncomfortable reality of daily life in the Middle Ages, and of a whole community – from Gatty, the reeve's daughter, to Tanwen, the chamber-servant, from Oliver, the priest, to Lady Alice, keeper of a terrible secret – as they face the conflicts and uncertainties of a new century.

The Seeing Stone is the first volume in the *Arthur* trilogy; books 2 and 3, *At the Crossing-Places* and *King of the Middle March* are also available.

GATTY'S TALE

A daring journey.
A death.
A dream.
A heroine you'll never forget.
Gatty, the field-girl beloved already by readers of the Arthur trilogy, is at the heart of this enthralling story. In the year 1203, nine companions set out from Wales on a great pilgrimage across Europe to Jerusalem. Not all of them will come home. Gatty is among them Eager, bold and resolute, wide open to new experiences, she has an extraordinary journey of her own to make.

By Michelle Paver

WOLF BROTHER

Torak is alone . . . wounded, terrified, and on the run.

An outcast like his father, he has avoided all contact with the clans.
But now his father lies dead: slaughtered by a demon in the form of
a great bear.

Somehow, Torak must keep going. His only ally is an orphaned
wolf cub.

Through the whispering spruce trees comes an evil more
terrible than any clan can imagine, and soon Torak must face a
foe he can neither outrun nor outwit: a foe who stalks him as
silently as breath.

Wolf Brother carries you back thousands of years to the ancient
darkness of the Forest: to a world steeped in natural magic and
elemental terror – a world in which trusting a friend means
risking your life . . .

Wolf Brother is the first book in the *Chronicles of Ancient
Darkness* series. *Spirit Walker, Soul Eater* and *Outcast*
are also available from Orion Children's Books.

By Caroline Lawrence

THE THIEVES OF OSTIA

The year is AD 79.

The place is Ostia, the port of Rome.

Flavia Gemina, a Roman sea captain's daughter, is about to embark o
a thrilling adventure.

The theft of her father's signet ring leads her to three extraordinary
people – Jonathan the Jewish boy next door, Nubia the African slave
girl, and Lupus, the mute beggar boy – who become her friends.
Their investigations take them to the harbour, the forum, and the
tombs of the dead, as they try to discover who is killing the dogs of
Ostia, and why.

The first of the Roman Mysteries is an exciting whodunnit that tells
you just what it was like to live in Ancient Rome. There are now
fourteen titles in the Roman Mysteries series – a further three are
planned.

THE ROMAN MYSTERIES
by Caroline Lawrence

Marcus Sedgwick

THE BOOK OF DEAD DAYS

The days between Christmas and New Year's Eve are dead days,
when spirits roam and magic shifts restlessly just beneath the surface of our lives. A lot can happen in
the dead days.

There is a magician called Valerian who must save his own life, or
pay the price for the pact he made with evil so many years ago.
But will alchemy and sorcery be any match against the demonic
power pursuing him? Helping him is his
servant, Boy, a child with no name and no past, and the quick-
witted Willow, and watching their fortune, mapping their
destinies . . . is Fate.

Set in dark, dangerous cities and in the frozen countryside of a
distant time and place *The Book of Dead Days*, beautifully
evoked and dramatic, conjures a spell-binding story of power,
corruption and desperate magic.

'a dark melodrama kept sharp by surprise.'
Julia Eccleshare, *Guardian*

The sequel to *The Book of Dead Days*, *The Dark Flight Down* is
also available from Orion Children's Books.